SHOWTYM ADVENTURES

DANDY, THE MOUNTAIN PONY

KELLY WILSON

SHOWTYM ADVENTURES

DANDY, THE MOUNTAIN PONY

PUFFIN

UK | USA | Canada | Ireland | Australia
India | New Zealand | South Africa | China

Puffin is an imprint of the Penguin Random House group of companies, whose addresses
can be found at global.penguinrandomhouse.com.

Penguin
Random House
New Zealand

First published by Penguin Random House New Zealand, 2017

10 9 8 7 6 5 4 3 2 1

Text © Kelly Wilson, 2017

The moral right of the author has been asserted.

Cover design by Cat Taylor © Penguin Random House New Zealand
Text design by Emma Jakicevich © Penguin Random House New Zealand
Illustrations by Heather Wilson © Penguin Random House New Zealand
Cover illustrations by Jenny Cooper © Penguin Random House New Zealand

Printed and bound in Australia by Griffin Press, an Accredited ISO AS/NZS 14001
Environmental Management Systems Printer

A catalogue record for this book is available from the National Library of New Zealand.

ISBN 978-0-14-377149-4
eISBN 978-0-14-377150-0

penguinrandomhouse.co.nz

MIX
Paper from
responsible sources
FSC® C009448

This book is dedicated to our parents.
Thank you for teaching us to follow our dreams, and that anything is possible if we work hard, make sacrifices and continuously strive for self-improvement. We wouldn't be where we are without the life lessons you instilled in us.

Growing up, we Wilson sisters — Vicki, Amanda and me (I'm Kelly) — were three ordinary girls with a love of horses and dreams of Grand Prix show jumping, taming wild horses and becoming world champions.

In *Showtym Adventures*, we want to share stories based on our early years with ponies, to inspire you to have big dreams too! I hope you enjoy reading about the special ponies that started us on our journey ...

Love,
    Kelly

Contents

Chapter 1
Goodbye, Lease Pony

"COME ON, BOY," VICKI WHISPERED to her pony, Cardiff. "If it's our last show together, let's make it a good one." Tears shone in her blue eyes as she groomed his sleek white coat, brushed his mane and oiled his hooves. She'd washed him three times to get the stains out and he'd never looked better.

She couldn't believe, after just one year together, his owner had sold him. Vicki had always hoped the owner would see how much she loved Cardiff and let her keep leasing him forever. She knew one day soon she'd outgrow the 12.2-hand pony — since she was already nine years old — but she'd imagined her little sisters, Kelly and Amanda, taking over the reins so he could stay in the family.

"Vicki, can you help me brush Charlie?" asked four-year-old Amanda, her youngest sister. Vicki glanced over to where Amanda sat balanced on a feed bucket, carefully picking out Charlie Brown's hooves. The flea-bitten grey pony was still covered in bits of hay and dirt, and they were due in the ring for Best Groomed in less than ten minutes.

With a sigh, Vicki turned to help, but seven-year-old Kelly beat her to it. "I'll help her," she said. "Twinkle's all ready, and anyway, you should be spending every second with Cardiff."

"Thanks," Vicki said, grateful for her sister's understanding. She returned to her pony and gently brushed his tail, careful not to pull out any of the precious strands of hair.

Soon all three ponies were bridled and ready. Although they were all grey and sized between 11 and 12.2 hands, that's where the similarities ended. Cardiff was a chunky gelding who'd quickly earned the paddock name 'Fatso' when he'd first joined their family. In comparison, Kelly's pony Twinkle was a pretty mare with delicate features, and Amanda's pony Charlie Brown, who both Vicki and Kelly had ridden when they were younger, was cheeky in both looks and personality.

Mum and Dad arrived back from the show office just before the Best Groomed class started and helped to tie the entry numbers onto the girls' arms.

"Enjoy today, kiddo," Dad said as he hugged Vicki good luck. "I'm sorry we couldn't afford to buy Cardiff for you, but don't let it take away from enjoying your last day together."

As Vicki waited in line for the judge to look over her pony, her mind wandered. She knew how stressed her parents were feeling, trying to work out a way to afford a new pony. Twinkle had cost just $75 and Charlie had been $250, but trying to scrape together even that much money was a struggle at the moment. There was no way they could have paid the thousands of dollars that Cardiff's new rider had paid for him.

Vicki thought back to when she'd first been given Cardiff. She'd felt so lucky when she'd been offered him on a free lease — she could never have had such a nice pony otherwise. In the year they'd been together, she'd enjoyed lots of success with him at Ribbon Days and in Pony Club events.

But now he was leaving, and Vicki desperately wanted a new pony so she could keep riding. Her sisters were being very kind and had offered to let her borrow their ponies, but Twinkle and Charlie seemed much too small now. Besides, Kelly and Amanda loved riding as much as she did, so she didn't want them to miss out. Her parents had told her that the right pony would come along — she just hoped it would be soon. She had dreams of being one of the best riders in the country but she knew she had lots to learn before that could ever become a reality.

"Vicki, stop day-dreaming — the judge is coming," whispered Kelly.

Shaking away her thoughts, Vicki turned to check Cardiff was standing with his legs square, then smiled as the judge approached. Carefully the judge ran her hands over the pony's coat, then picked up his hooves to check they were clean. With a satisfied smile, she turned to Vicki and said, "You're a lucky girl — he's a beautiful pony. You've done a wonderful job presenting him."

As the judge moved along to Kelly, then Amanda, Vicki turned to Cardiff with a wobbly smile. She whispered in his ear, "I have been lucky — thank you for the best year ever."

Soon the judge was finished and called the winners forward. Vicki was in first place, and she proudly led her pony to collect his red ribbon. Neither of her sisters placed, but Vicki wasn't surprised. Although they loved their ponies, they didn't take their riding as seriously as she did. Unlike her, they hadn't spent hours polishing their boots and cleaning their gear in preparation for the show, nor had they washed their ponies, who were more yellow than white. Their mum said it was because they were younger than her and weren't used to competing, but Vicki just thought they were lazy.

U U U

For the rest of the day, Vicki and Cardiff continued their winning streak. By the end of the show he'd won so many ribbons that they didn't fit on his short, stocky neck. Trophies spilled out of Vicki's arms, and rosettes hung off Cardiff's bridle. It was the perfect last ride on her special pony, and that night she dreamed of what her next pony might look like.

Chapter 2
The Mountain Stallion

A MONTH AFTER SHE'D HAD to say goodbye to Cardiff, Vicki was still without a pony. Every day she would search the newspaper for ponies advertised for sale, but her family had been able to scrape together only a couple of hundred dollars, and there was nothing in their price range. With each day that passed Vicki felt more disheartened.

One day after school, her parents told her they had a surprise trip planned. "We're going to see some wild ponies!" her mum said with a huge smile.

"Real wild horses?" squealed Kelly.

"Where?" Vicki asked in confusion. "I didn't know there were wild ponies around here."

"Neither did we," her dad said, "but there's a herd that runs wild on a mountain, just fifteen minutes from here. Look what I saw in today's paper!"

Vicki reached for the newspaper, unable to believe what she was hearing. Right there, in black and white, her dad had circled the following words: *Wild mountain ponies, $50 each.*

With shaking hands, she re-read the words, then looked up at her parents. "My favourite books are about taming wild horses," she whispered.

Mum leant over and ruffled Vicki's long brown hair. "I know they are. Maybe you'll find your own one to tame. We've already phoned the people and they're expecting us to look at the ponies this afternoon."

"Hurry up, let's go!" Amanda cried, with a stamp of her foot. "I've been waiting all day for you and Kelly to come home from school."

Excited, Vicki, Kelly and Amanda pulled on their boots and piled into the family's old car. As their dad drove, the chatter of the three sisters filled the air, their excitement contagious as they neared the old volcano, which loomed above the Hikurangi Swamp.

∪ ∪ ∪

Their car rattled to a stop at the end of a steep gravel driveway. A lady met them and led the family higher up the mountain, walking up a winding bush track that weaved between trees and volcanic rocks.

"How long have the wild ponies lived up here?" Vicki asked.

"Our family has been breeding Welsh ponies on this mountain for generations," the lady said. "It's only in recent years we haven't been able to keep up with training them. Now the herd roams wild — some of them have never been touched."

"How many are there?" Vicki said, eager to learn as much as possible about the ponies.

"There must be about twenty or thirty now — I've lost track of all the foals that have been born over the years. Whoever takes them will have a hard time catching them, let alone taming them."

After they'd been walking for ten minutes, the

trees thinned out and the track opened out into a volcanic crater. The grass was sparse from over-grazing, and dozens of ponies dotted the landscape.

The family paused at the edge of the trees. As they watched, a beautiful chestnut pony pranced

down the hill, his glistening red coat rippling like lava and his long mane flowing in the wind. With a shrill cry he screamed a challenge to a palomino stallion who stood grazing with his mares.

Coming to a halt, the chestnut rose on his hind

legs, his forelegs striking the air. Vicki gasped as the palomino rushed forward with teeth bared and chased the younger stallion away. With a loud snort the chestnut leapt to safety and darted up into the trees, disappearing from sight.

"Why were they fighting?" asked Amanda. "Won't they hurt each other?"

"It's the way of wild horses," the lady replied. "The young chestnut stallion wants a herd of his own, and the palomino has to fight to protect his mares from being stolen."

Turning, she pointed to the palomino and his small herd. "Everything in this herd is available if you're interested. The stallion is six years old, the grey mare with the foal is about eight and . . ."

Vicki listened distractedly as the lady pointed out more ponies for sale, her eyes fixed on the trees, hoping the chestnut stallion would reappear. Quietly, she asked, "What about the chestnut?"

The lady looked down at her with a cautious expression on her face and said, "They're brothers, you know. But they are nothing alike. The palomino is curious and sensible, but the chestnut is a troublemaker. He's only four years old, but he's going to be a hard one to tame."

"But we could choose him, if he was our favourite?"

"I certainly wouldn't recommend him, but yes, he also has to go, one way or another."

"Can we please go closer to the horses?" Amanda asked, tugging on the lady's arm.

"Follow me," she replied, striding ahead.

Vicki's gaze returned to the tree-line, but the elusive chestnut was nowhere to be seen.

As they drew closer, the palomino raised his head, his flowing white mane contrasting with the golden hues of his coat. A white blaze ran down his nose. "He's the most beautiful pony I've ever seen," Kelly said, jumping up and down and clapping her hands in excitement. Startled, the palomino leapt back, circling his herd to put more distance between them.

"Don't you know anything about wild horses?" Vicki said, furious that her sister had spooked the curious stallion. "You have to stay quiet and move slowly so you don't scare them."

Kelly dropped her gaze and slowly shuffled back behind her mum. "I've never seen a wild horse before — how was I supposed to know?"

As they watched the herd, the grey mare stepped forward. Every rib was showing, and her hip bones were jutting through her taut hide. Her foal bunted her playfully, trying to suckle.

"It's been a hard year," the lady sighed. "They'll starve this winter if I don't reduce numbers."

Finally, sensing movement in the trees, Vicki turned and saw a flash of red. "Mum, Dad," she said urgently. "He's watching us."

They saw the young chestnut stallion, standing alert and peering out from the shadow of the trees.

"Everyone else wait here while Vicki and I get a closer look at him," her mum said.

Slowly, they made their way up the hill towards the chestnut. With each of their steps Vicki could see the stallion tense, his neck arched as he snorted in fear.

"I've never seen a pony like him," Vicki whispered, her eyes wide.

"He sure is something," her mum agreed, as the stallion tossed his head and galloped past them down the hillside, the pounding of his hooves echoing around the crater.

As they made their way back to the others, Vicki

kept her eyes on the fleeing pony. None of the others were as beautiful, strong or splendid as the chestnut stallion, and already her heart was set on taming him.

As they hiked back down the mountain to their car, Vicki dreamed of everything she'd be able to do with him once she won his trust. Taming a wild, untouched stallion was everything she'd ever dreamed of. Now she just had to convince her parents she could do it.

Chapter 3
If Wishes Were Horses...

THAT NIGHT, WHEN VICKI'S PARENTS came to tuck her into bed, in the small room she shared with her sisters, all she could talk about was the wild mountain ponies. "It would be a dream to tame the chestnut stallion. You know how hard it is to find nice ponies that we can afford — they're always too old, or too young, or injured, or difficult. I never thought owning a pony that beautiful would be possible."

"There's a very good reason they're so cheap," her dad cautioned. "Taming wild horses is much more difficult than it sounds in the books you read."

"Especially the chestnut. It's in his nature to fight — didn't you see the way he was baiting his brother?" her mum added. "What about the palomino? He looks much easier."

But Vicki was adamant. The chestnut stallion was the right pony for her. "Please, Mum and Dad — you know I'm good with naughty ponies. I really think I can tame him."

"I believe you, kiddo," her dad said. "Now convince your mum while I go say goodnight to Amanda and Kelly."

"We just don't want to see you get hurt," Vicki's mum said. "I know you did a great job retraining Charlie when you first got him, and helping Kelly with Twinkle, but that's nothing compared to the challenges you'll face working with a wild horse."

"You've ridden ever since you were a little girl," Vicki argued. "I'm sure you can teach me everything I need to know."

Laughing, her mum replied, "I rode farm horses and stroppy thoroughbreds off the racetrack — I don't think they're quite the same thing. Besides, I've barely ridden since you kids got your own ponies.

I'm out of practice."

Tugging on her mum's arm, Vicki leant forward. "Don't you miss it? I'd be so sad if I couldn't ride — it's my favourite thing in the world."

With a wistful smile, her mum gave her a hug good night. "Sometimes, but there's not enough money for all our dreams to come true," she whispered in her daughter's ear as she leant forward to hug her.

U U U

Unable to sleep, Vicki mulled over her mum's last words, convinced they had a hidden meaning. Did her mum want to ride again? If so, was it only money that stopped her?

After a restless sleep, Vicki dragged herself out of bed the next morning and ran down the hallway of their tiny house.

"Mum, why don't you ride anymore?" Vicki demanded.

Surprised, her mum glanced up from the clothes she was mending. When she saw her daughter's determined face she put down the needle and thread. "It's not my passion anymore. You and your sisters are what's most important to me now."

"But if we had enough money, would you have your own horse again?"

"But we don't," her mum said with a sigh. "Sometimes there's no point imagining what might be. I get more than enough pleasure watching you and your sisters ride."

"Mum, we budgeted two hundred dollars for a new pony and the wild ones are only fifty dollars each. Couldn't we both get one? The skinny grey mare would be big enough for you to ride."

Shaking her head, her mum replied, "If we take one of the wild ponies it will cost a fortune to feed for the first few months. The cost of hay alone will chip away at the last of our savings. And since we don't have high enough fences to keep a horse like that contained, we'd have to keep them at the neighbours'."

Vicki sighed and her shoulders drooped. She turned to the kitchen to make her breakfast.

As she sat at the table she glanced outside, where Kelly and Amanda were feeding Twinkle and Charlie. She felt a pang of envy that her sisters still had ponies to look after. Vicki felt sure her mum wanted to ride again, and although she had her heart set on the chestnut stallion, she felt bad that her mum had to miss out.

"Mum, what if you spend the money on one of the wild ponies for yourself? I can wait until we save up again, or maybe a lease pony will become available," she said.

"Honey, I've had a whole lifetime with horses. I'm not going to let you miss out on having your own pony. If it's a wild stallion you want, we'll make it happen. I want you to grow up having all your dreams come true."

Glancing at her mother hopefully, Vicki whispered, "The chestnut one?"

"Let me talk to your dad," her mum replied. "In the meantime, go round up Kelly and get ready for school. Education is even more important than riding, and there's no way you're going to be late!"

∪ ∪ ∪

That afternoon, when her mum picked them up from

school, Vicki had a smile a mile wide. She'd spent the whole day brainstorming the pony problem, and she hadn't focused on anything her teacher had been saying.

"I have the perfect plan, Mum," she said excitedly. "Like I said, we should get two wild horses — one for you and one for me — then we can train them together!"

Her mum shook her head. "We already talked about this — there's no grass in the yards and the cost of hay is too high. We can't afford to feed two ponies, and it's not fair for them to lose even more condition. You saw how thin the grey mare was."

"But what if they don't need hay?" said Vicki. "What if we cut grass from the roadsides and fill up wheelbarrows to feed them with? I already asked Kelly and she said she'd be happy to help." She looked back at her two little sisters sitting in the back seat of the car. "You'll help too, right, Amanda?" Amanda grinned and nodded.

Vicki's mum was speechless, but then she had to admit it was a great idea.

"You're a clever one, Vicki. I'll talk to your dad and see if he thinks it could work."

With a grin, Vicki settled into her seat and did up her seatbelt. She couldn't wait to get home and ask Dad.

Chapter 4
Not One, But Four

As soon as the car was parked, all three sisters jumped out and hurried to find their father. He was in their bird aviary, fixing a hole a rabbit had dug under the fence. Vicki opened the door, careful not to let any birds escape like she'd accidentally done in the past.

The aviary was almost as big as their house, with an arch of huge volcanic boulders in the centre. Underneath the rocks their pet rabbits had made tunnels to play in, and on hot days the guinea pigs lazed in the shade. Overhead, birds of every size and colour squawked: doves, finches, canaries, rosellas and budgies.

While she watched her dad work, Vicki told him about the plan she'd come up with. Her dad put down his tools. "Your mum will be so pleased — she's often talked about getting another horse, without knowing how to make it happen. This is a great idea!"

"Since I'm so clever, can I pretty please get the chestnut, Dad? I just know he'll be a champion one day," Vicki said, cheekily.

She watched her dad's face grow thoughtful, then break into a grin. "The chestnut it is," he said. "No daughter of mine is going to be stopped from living her dreams."

"Really, Dad?" said Vicki, clasping her hand over her mouth in delight.

"Yes. I'll ring and we'll arrange a time to round them up."

Unable to contain her excitement, Vicki grabbed her dad's hand and dragged him back to the house. As soon as she burst through the door she shouted, "He said yes!"

She watched as her mum's eyes grew wide. Kelly

and Amanda rushed into the house and started jumping up and down, asking their mum which of the wild horses she would choose.

"It'll have to be the grey," she said. "She's one of the few big enough for me to ride, and I'll rest better at night knowing she'll have good grass this winter."

Dad glanced around at his girls, then said very seriously, "I really liked the palomino stallion. Do you think you can pick enough grass for three wild horses?"

With a screech Kelly ran to him, holding out her arms. "You're not serious, Dad?" she shrieked. "He's my favourite!"

With a laugh, he tossed her in the air and caught her again. "I happen to know a thing or two about horses. You can help me tame him, Kelly, but he won't be with us forever. We'll sell him to help pay the the extra costs of having two new ponies to care for."

Nodding her head frantically, Kelly grinned in agreement. "That's OK, Dad. I love Twinkle too much to want another pony, and besides, I'd be too scared to ride a wild stallion."

Setting her back down on the ground, her dad smiled. "You never know, Kelly — one day you'll be big and brave enough to tame one."

Stamping her foot in agitation, Amanda tugged on her mum's arm.

"What about me? I want to help tame a wild horse too!" she cried. Glancing down at the four-year-old, who was on the verge of throwing a tantrum, her mum fought to stop a smile from escaping. "I think you need to grow up a little before you get a wild pony."

"Yeah," said Vicki. "You're too small. The horses might trample you by mistake."

Furious, Amanda turned on her sister. "I am *not* small!"

"Amanda, I'm sure you can help *all* of us," Dad said, with a warning glance at Vicki.

Reaching for the phone, he dialled the number of the lady who owned the ponies. There was a sudden hush as they listened to him talk. At one point his face took on a worried expression and he left the room. The rest of the family waited nervously for him to return.

"Apparently the grey mare's foal is too young to wean," he said as he stepped back into the room which was the parents' bedroom, dining room and kitchen all rolled into one.

With a sigh, the girls' mother put on a brave face. "Maybe it's just not meant to be," she said.

Shaking his head, their father grinned as if he was struggling to keep a secret. "We are the proud owners of four wild ponies!" he announced. Looking at Amanda, he added, "How do you feel about helping us tame that golden filly? Think you're up to it?"

Looking overwhelmed, Amanda glanced around the room. "Maybe I'd be too scared," she whispered.

Mum tugged her onto her lap. "Don't you worry, Amanda — foals are too little to do much training. Mostly they just eat and grow. Dad and I can help get her haltered and you just have to feed her grass and talk to her lots until she's your best friend." Turning to her husband, she drew her daughters closer. "How are we going to afford this?" she asked in a worried tone.

"The owner agreed to $175 including the foal, so it'll use up most of our savings," he said. "I guess it'll come down to how well we train them, because we'll have to sell both the palominos at some point. Hopefully they bring in enough money to cover the costs of having extra ponies on the property."

Chapter 5
The Round-Up

THE NEXT WEEK WAS SPENT preparing for the arrival of the wild ponies. While Vicki and Kelly were at school and Amanda was at kindy, their parents would drive to the mountain to repair the yards there, to make sure they were sturdy enough to hold the wild horses. In the evenings Vicki and her sisters would help by getting the neighbours' stockyards ready.

"Vicki, come over here and hold this rail level so I can nail it in," her dad called.

In the next yard over, Kelly helped her mum fill

up water troughs — old blue drums sawed in half especially for the wild horses to drink from. And it was Amanda's job to collect any large rocks and toss them under the fence. They didn't want the wild ponies to get stone bruises on their hooves.

"Mum, what happens if the wild horses don't want to be caught?" Kelly asked. "Maybe they like living on the mountain."

After giving the question some serious thought, Mum answered. "The lady desperately needs them gone, and if we don't take them, someone else will. At least if they come home with us we know they'll get lots of love."

Nodding her head in agreement, Kelly giggled. "Lots of love — and lots of hand-picked grass."

∪ ∪ ∪

Soon everything was ready, and the Saturday of the big round-up finally arrived. Piling into their little green and red horse truck, the family headed up to the mountain.

At the old yards, which were off to one side of

the crater, some friends of the family were already waiting to help with the muster. Dad quickly took charge and outlined his plan.

"Vicki, you stay under the trees over there and look after your sisters while we round up the horses."

Vicki was annoyed at being left behind. "I'm happy to help. Why can't I join in on the action?"

Distracted, her dad pointed to the tree-line. "Trees. Now."

Slinking off, Vicki grabbed her sisters' hands. "Come on, we'll make our own fun."

As soon as all the adults had set off to round up the wild ponies, Vicki challenged her sisters to a tree-climbing competition.

"We'll have a much better view from up high," she said. Grabbing a branch, she swung herself up into a tree and waited for her sisters to join her. Kelly quickly followed, but Amanda was too little to reach the lowest branch.

"Hang on a second," said Vicki as she jumped out of the tree and got down onto her hands and knees. "Climb on my back."

Soon all three sisters were in the tree. Amanda carefully settled herself on the lowest branch while

Vicki and Kelly climbed higher.

"The ponies are coming!" cried Amanda.

Unable to see through the leaves, Vicki quickly scurried back down. "Can you see my chestnut?"

"I can't tell, there's heaps of chestnuts!"

Settling on the branch beside Amanda, Vicki and Kelly watched the first herd of horses canter into the yards. Among them were the palomino stallion and his grey mare and foal. Behind them, Vicki watched as her mum rushed forward to shut the gate. The chestnut was nowhere to be seen.

Jumping out of the tree, she hurried over to her parents, distraught.

"What if the chestnut's hiding in the trees again and you can't find him?"

"We'll find him eventually, I'm sure," her dad replied. He moved off to herd the ponies into the back yard, and reopened the main gate for more horses to come through.

Vicki watched as they set off in search of the chestnut, the only pony they still needed to find. Returning to the tree to wait with her sisters, she snapped small twigs off the branches blocking her view.

"Stop fiddling," Kelly snapped.

"I've made so many plans about how to win the chestnut's trust and all the shows we're going to do together, but what happens if he can't be caught?"

"Killing the tree is not going to help."

Yawning, Amanda stretched her arms. "Why don't we think of names for our ponies? Otherwise I might fall asleep."

"Great idea," Kelly said. "What about Lava for the chestnut? He's the right colour and he lives on a volcano."

"What's lava?" Amanda asked.

"Something I learnt about at school. You know, it's the hot rock that comes out when a volcano erupts."

"That's a stupid name for a stallion," Vicki grumbled. "Besides, I can't choose a name until I get to know his personality. Or if he's even going to be mine."

∪ ∪ ∪

Over half an hour passed, and Vicki became more and more despondent. Below her, Amanda and

Kelly chased each other through the trees, playing hide and seek. Then a movement caught her eye, and in the distance she saw another group of ponies approaching.

"Amanda, Kelly!" she called. "Keep still so you don't scare the ponies."

Watching urgently, she kept an eye out for the chestnut. She froze when she saw his unmistakable white blaze.

Soon more than twenty horses paced frantically around the yards, and the sorting process began. Vicki watched anxiously as her pony was sorted into a yard by himself. Next the palomino stallion and the grey mare and her foal were drafted out into another yard, and then the main gate was opened and the rest of the horses were set free. Leaping through the gate, they galloped across the crater, desperate to put distance between themselves and the people who had kept them captive.

Stressed, the chestnut stallion whinnied, his loud, piercing cry filling the air as he called out to the fleeing horses. Sweat broke out on his coat and his eyes gleamed fire. A deep feeling of pity filled Vicki as she watched the stallion pace within the confinement of the fences. She could never have dreamed a horse could have so much spirit, and she desperately hoped she would be able to tame him.

In the next yard over, the palomino stallion stood alert but calm. Vicki turned to Kelly.

"Maybe I chose the wrong pony," she whispered.

Patting her on the leg, Kelly shook her head.

"You're the bravest rider of us all. Ever since you were little you rode Twinkle and Charlie when they were being naughty, and before that, Samson and Bella," she said, rattling off the names of all the horses they'd owned. "Even Cardiff misbehaved when you got him, and you trained him into the perfect pony. You'll be fine."

Unable to shake her doubts, Vicki watched the ponies get herded onto the waiting horse truck. It would be the chestnut's last time roaming on the volcanic mountain. Taming him was going to be a big challenge.

Chapter 6
The Hard Yards

FIFTEEN MINUTES LATER, the horse truck pulled into the driveway of their neighbours' farm. Vicki watched as the wild ponies hesitantly stepped down the ramp and into the waiting yards. The mare and foal were kept together, but both stallions were yarded separately.

As the chestnut stallion snorted and plunged down the raceway into his yard, he seemed to catch Vicki's eye. If ever she'd seen hate expressed by a horse, she saw it then. Filled with guilt, she stepped down from the fence and turned away. She felt terrible for taking a stallion that was used to living free and imprisoning him in a small yard.

"He hates it here," she said quietly to her mum.

"He's just confused and scared from leaving the only home he's ever known. Give him time to settle. And no matter what — don't enter his yard, it's not safe." Glancing over at Amanda and Kelly, Mum added, "That goes for all of you. I don't want to see anyone going into the yards. It's OK to watch the ponies or hold out handfuls of grass through the

fence, but don't you dare mistake them for quiet kids' ponies," she said, holding up a stern finger.

Hoping her mum was right, Vicki returned to the yard. She sat on the top rail and watched the chestnut stallion as he paced.

"You'll be OK, boy," she whispered. "Everything will be just fine and dandy, you wait and see."

"I think that's a great name for him," her dad said. Startled, Vicki swung her head around.

"What name?" Vicki asked, confused.

"Just Fine 'n' Dandy," he replied. "It'll be good for him to hear you tell him everything is going to be OK whenever you call his name."

Looking back at her pony, Vicki tried it out.

"Is that what you want to be called?" she asked. "Just Fine 'n' Dandy?" To her shock, the stallion pricked an ear and raised his striking head, looking directly at her. "He likes it," said Vicki, smiling.

"Yes, he does," her dad agreed. "I'm sure he'll settle in just fine."

"What are you going to call your stallion, Dad?" Vicki asked.

"Exquisite. Kelly came up with it," he replied. "But I think we'll call him Squizzy for short."

"It suits him," smiled Vicki. "He looks much more relaxed than Dandy."

"And your Mum has named the grey mare Jude — but she hasn't named the foal yet."

Impatient, Amanda suddenly called out, "Hurry up, Vicki! I'm hungry and Mum said we can't go home for dinner until the horses have been fed."

Vicki jumped down from the fence and followed the rest of her family down the long, winding driveway and out to the road, where the grass grew the longest.

"How much will the horses eat?" Vicki asked, as she snipped handful after handful of grass.

"We'll start with a wheelbarrow for each horse twice a day, but if it's all gone in the morning we might have to do more."

"It's much slower than I thought it would be," complained Amanda.

"No complaints," growled Dad. "We made a commitment to feed four horses, and we always knew it was going to be a lot of work. Complaining about it won't make the time pass any faster."

With a yawn, Amanda returned to tugging at the grass, her movements sluggish with exhaustion.

Finally the first wheelbarrow was full, and Dad raced it up the driveway and emptied it into Dandy's yard. They filled up the wheelbarrow again and again for the other horses, not finishing until after the sun had set.

"Good job, girls," their mum said. "It's been a long day, but worth it, don't you think?"

Looking over at Dandy happily munching on the grass, Vicki had to agree.

"You always taught us that dreams could come true if we worked hard enough. I have a feeling Dandy is going to be worth it."

"Remember that when we're out here picking grass in the rain next week!" Dad said.

U U U

Vicki and her sisters slept in the next morning.

"The ponies are waiting for their breakfast," their mum called, as she banged on the wall to wake them.

With a groan, Kelly looked at the clock beside her bed. She pulled a pillow over her head and grumbled, 'But it's still night-time!"

Vicki saw sunlight peeking through the curtains and jumped out of bed, hurriedly pulling on her clothes.

"It's eight o'clock! Hurry up, guys — Dandy will be hungry!" she said.

A few minutes later, Amanda wandered into the kitchen and stretched sleepily before grabbing a bowl and asking her mum to make her breakfast. Whisking it away from her, Dad turned her in the direction of the door.

"There's a new rule in this house: no one gets to eat until the horses are fed."

Amanda dragged her feet. "But I'm starving, and I won't be able to work if I'm hungry."

Vicki smirked. Amanda loved her food and always got a little angry when she was hungry. "No complaining, remember?"

Looking around, Mum asked, "Where's Kelly?"

"Tell her she's got ten seconds to be in the car," Dad replied.

52

The morning routine took even longer than the night before — not only did they have to pick grass, but their parents also had to muck out the manure from the yards, moving quietly so the horses wouldn't get frightened. The palomino and the grey mare and her foal were quite settled, but Dandy started panicking as soon as Dad opened the gate.

'Woah, boy," he said. "I'm not here to hurt you."

"He looks like he's going to jump the fence," Vicki said nervously, as she watched from the laneway.

"I don't think he's ready for me to enter his yard. How about we move him into the next one over so I can muck out?" Dad opened another gate and slowly stepped around Dandy to encourage him into the opening. Seeing an opportunity to escape, Dandy darted into the next yard and stood trembling while the gate was relatched.

"Come in and help me, Vicki," Dad said. "The sooner we get his yard clean, the quicker he can return and get settled."

Kelly and Amanda helped their mum cut grass, emptying it into the yards for the horses to eat. Once they were done the family sat on the fence overlooking the horses, talking quietly to their new steeds. Their quiet voices lulled the ponies and they stood quietly eating.

Eventually all the jobs were finished and the family headed home for breakfast. Vicki felt as if she was half-starved and ate twice as much as normal. She was desperate to return to the yards to work with the horses. During the weeks there wouldn't be much daylight in the evenings after school.

When they returned to the yards soon after lunch, Vicki was disheartened to see the horses had eaten all their grass.

"We can't let the horses go that long without food, so we're going to have to feed them three times a day," Mum said. "You girls can help on weekends, but Dad and I will do the lunch feeds on school days."

With a few groans, the girls collected the wheelbarrow and headed down to the road to cut more grass. It looked like they would be spending over two hours every day just cutting grass.

"No wonder people normally feed hay to horses!" said Vicki.

"If we were feeding hay they'd go through at least two slices each, three times a day. That's fifteen bales every week, so it quickly adds up."

"Ouch!" said Vicki, quickly doing the maths. "We'd be spending more on hay in one week than it cost to buy the ponies."

Her dad nodded. "We could never have afforded that, so thank you for your genius idea to cut grass."

When they finished, Vicki settled down to watch Dandy eat.

"So, how do we tame them, anyway?" she asked her mum.

"I have no idea," she replied softly. "Let's just take it one day at a time and let the horses be our teachers."

Chapter 7
Baby Steps

OVER THE NEXT FEW DAYS Vicki, Kelly and Amanda fell into a routine. They would wake up at 7 a.m. and head down to the stockyards to cut grass for the wild horses, then head home for breakfast. It was always a rush for Vicki and Kelly to get dressed and ready for school in time, and they were often late.

Arriving after the bell for the third day in a row, Vicki hurried into class, pulling grass from her hair.

"Sorry I'm late," she said as she passed her teacher a note.

"Please excuse Vicki for being late, it couldn't

be helped," she read. "You've used the same excuse three days in a row and it certainly doesn't offer much information. What exactly is causing you to be late?"

"I'm taming a wild stallion, and I have to pick grass for him each morning."

With a frown, the teacher locked eyes with Vicki. "As amusing as that sounds, you are required to tell me the truth."

"It's true, I promise. Last weekend we caught four wild ponies in the mountains. They're staying at the neighbours' until they're tame enough to bring home," Vicki said.

"Next time you're late I want to talk to your parents," the teacher said sternly. "Now go to your seat."

∪ ∪ ∪

The 3 p.m. bell never came quickly enough. As soon as it rang, Vicki sprinted to the school entrance, closely followed by Kelly. Their parents always came prepared with a change of clothes and a snack, so they could go straight to the ponies.

Once they got to the yards, they had only an hour to spend with the horses. The rest of the time was spent cutting grass, mucking out or topping up the ponies' water, so they could get home before dark. Dandy was still too wild to work with, so each day Vicki would just sit on the rails, quietly chatting to him.

"One day we're going to be best friends," she told the wild stallion. "I know you think I'm scary right now, but soon you'll realise how much fun we can have. We'll go on farm rides and learn to jump logs and ditches, then how to jump over walls and show-jumps. If you're really good, you can even come to Pony Club camp and swim at the beach — you'll love that."

Each day, Vicki talked non-stop for the full hour, sharing her hopes and dreams with Dandy. Mostly he just ignored her and stood tense. But on Thursday, five days after he'd been mustered from the mountain, Vicki finally noticed a change come over him.

"Am I boring you?" she asked in surprise, when she noticed the pony yawn. "It's good you're finally relaxed enough to sleep when I'm around. You rest while I go check on the other ponies."

Climbing down, Vicki was surprised to see her dad in the yard with the palomino stallion, while Kelly watched intently from the fence. He stood about a metre away from him, holding out a handful of grass. Although the horse wasn't brave enough to step forward, he had his beautiful head outstretched.

"That's a good boy, Squizzy," Dad murmured. "You're a brave one, aren't you?" Dropping his hand, he slowly backed away from the horse until he stood near Kelly and Vicki. "If you think that's good, you should watch your mum working with Jude. She's already eating out of your mum's hand!"

Vicki's jaw dropped. She moved over to the next yard, careful to walk slowly so she didn't spook the ponies. Her dad was right: the mare stood in the yard beside Mum, greedily eating grass out of her mum's hands. The foal still hid behind her, unsure if humans were friends or not.

To Vicki's surprise, she could see heaps of cut grass still lying nearby in a blue drum. That meant Jude wasn't eating from her mum's hands because she was hungry and had no other choice, but because the horse trusted her. How she wished Dandy was already at that stage.

U U U

The next day Vicki watched enviously as her mum stroked Jude's neck for the first time. The mare was shocked by the contact and jumped backwards, but soon stepped forward and let herself be touched again. Even Squizzy was making good progress and was now stepping forward to eat out of her dad's hands.

The only horse that hadn't improved was Dandy, and Vicki was getting more and more worried that he was too wild to tame. Disheartened, she sat overlooking his yard, watching him.

"What am I supposed to do with you?" she said. "Don't you want to be my friend? The sooner you're tamed, the sooner you can come home. You'll love it at home. There's a big paddock to roam in and you'll get to know Charlie and Twinkle — they are heaps of fun, and I'm sure they'll teach you lots of good habits. Charlie used to be so naughty! He tried every dirty trick in the book to make me fall off when I first got him, but now he's perfect to ride. Even Amanda is safe on him, and she's only little."

Vicki was so caught up in her thoughts that she didn't even notice that Dandy had stepped closer until she heard him snort. Looking up in shock, she watched as the spirited stallion halted in the centre of the yard, facing her, no longer hiding in the furthest corner. Barely able to breathe, Vicki was careful to keep still.

"See, I'm not as scary as you think," she whispered. Unsettled, Dandy tossed his head, his long mane flying as he spun around and retreated to the corner again.

Jumping down from the rails, Vicki darted over to where the others stood.

"Mum, Dad, did you see that?" she gushed. "It's the first time he's taken a step towards me!"

"That's the way, Vicki," her mum said proudly. "Patience is key. We'll make a wild-horse tamer out of you yet!"

That night Vicki dreamed she and Dandy were galloping over the hills on the farm, outrunning lava as it spilled from the angry volcano above. Rocks were tossed out of the sky, thudding to earth in front of them. If they were too big to jump, Dandy would weave around them. On and on they galloped, his swiftness more than a match for the liquid fire that chased them.

Chapter 8
The Apple

THE NEXT MORNING Vicki woke up excited. It was the weekend again, which meant they'd be able to spend all day with the ponies. The timing couldn't have been better. She was sure Dandy would only improve now after his brave first steps yesterday.

For the first time, Dandy didn't panic when her dad walked into his yard to muck out. Vicki grinned. "He's getting better."

"He certainly is," her dad agreed. "Whatever you've been doing, keep it up."

Once the wheelbarrows of grass had been cut and

the horses fed, Vicki settled onto the fence again, talking away.

"You know, one day I'm going to be a Grand Prix showjumper," she said confidently. "I've jumped up to 75 centimetres so far, but I bet you'll be able to jump higher than that. I dreamt we were jumping over volcanic boulders last night and it felt like we were flying."

As Vicki talked, the stallion lifted his head from his food and turned to look at her. "I know you don't trust me yet," she whispered, "but I promise I'm not here to hurt you."

∪ ∪ ∪

"I don't understand why we can't spend the whole day at the yards," Vicki complained after breakfast.

"You've lived and breathed those wild horses since they arrived a week ago," her mum said. "You need to head outside and have an adventure. Go ride Charlie and Twinkle, or explore the river, but until I see the three of you girls having fun together, we're not going back to the yards."

Sulking, Vicki went in search of her sisters. It seemed boring having to play, when the real adventure was taming the wild horses. As she searched for Kelly and Amanda she came up with a plan.

"Do you guys want to ride out on the farm and have a picnic lunch?" she asked her sisters. "Kelly, you ride Twinkle, and Amanda and I can double on Charlie."

"That sounds like fun," Amanda said.

"You guys catch the ponies and I'll go pack some food," said Vicki as she hurried back towards the house.

Ten minutes later they were ready to go. Vicki had filled a backpack with apples and sandwiches, and Amanda and Kelly had the ponies waiting. Jumping on, bareback and with a halter, they rode down the road before crossing the bridge and heading towards the neighbour's farm.

Urging the ponies forward, they broke into a canter, racing each other up the first hill. But at the top, instead of turning the normal way through the gate and heading up the steepest hill, Vicki rode into a side paddock, past a shed and along a laneway.

"Where are we going? We never come this way,"

Kelly said, confused.

Smiling mischievously, Vicki told her to keep up. "You'll see soon enough!"

A few minutes later, they turned the final bend and in front of them were the stockyards. As soon as the wild ponies saw them, they started neighing and pacing the fence-line.

"I didn't even know we *could* ride here," Kelly said. "Do Mum and Dad know where we are?"

"No, but we won't stay long," Vicki promised. "I just want to spend a little more time with Dandy. He's so far behind Squizzy and Jude."

The girls quickly dismounted and put their ponies in the spare yard beside Dandy. The young stallion was very curious about the new arrivals and arched his neck, whinnying a challenge. Nervously, Charlie and Twinkle backed away.

Suddenly Dandy spun and kicked the fence, splintering the middle rail. Panicked, Vicki dashed into the yard and grabbed Twinkle and Charlie's halters.

"Hurry, Kelly — bring me their lead ropes. We need to get them away!"

The girls led their ponies out into the paddock

and tied them each to a post, careful to get the rope just the right length — not so long that they could get their hooves caught, but just long enough for them to be able to graze. Once they were secure, the girls rushed back to the yards to check on Dandy, relieved to see he had settled a little.

"How come Dandy didn't like Charlie?" Amanda asked with a frown. "Everyone likes Charlie!"

"I'm not sure," replied Vicki. "But next time we'll know to be more careful."

Settling down on the fence above Dandy's yard, Vicki opened her backpack and handed out sandwiches, then set the apples on the post beside them for later. As the girls munched they watched Dandy pace the fence-line, keeping a careful eye on the ponies in the distance. By the time they finished eating, he had finally relaxed and turned instead to watch them.

"Don't move," whispered Amanda. "Dandy's walking towards us right now."

Careful to keep still, Vicki lifted her gaze to watch the stallion prance towards them, stopping just a metre away and snorting. Raising a powerful foreleg, he pawed the ground before taking another step forward. It was the closest the stallion had ever been and Vicki could see a hard glint in his eye as he stretched out his neck.

"He's going to bite us!" Amanda whispered.

Gripping her sister's arm tightly, Vicki shook her head. "Don't you dare scare him. Keep still," she said, quietly but forcefully.

Stretching his neck as far as possible, Dandy leant forward, flattening back his ears and snaking his head. His powerful teeth flashed as he sunk his teeth into the apple beside them before darting backwards.

Terrified, Amanda burst into tears. "I thought he was going to eat me!"

"He just wanted the apple. You're OK," Kelly comforted her.

Too distracted watching her pony eat the apple, Vicki barely noticed Amanda crying. But when her sister went to grab the two remaining apples, Vicki shook her head.

"Leave them for Dandy. He seems to like them."

Chapter 9
First Touch

EACH DAY AFTER THAT, Vicki would bring an apple down to the yards and leave it on the post beside her while she talked to her pony. Every time, Dandy would step forward and eat it. Usually he would quickly retreat, but on the third day he stayed there and ate it, keeping a wary eye on Vicki.

"Well done, Vicki," her mum said as she watched from the laneway. "You're starting to win his trust."

"He's come so far," Vicki said proudly.

"I think he's ready for the next stage. Try holding out an apple and see if he'll eat it from your hand."

Slowly, Vicki held out an apple, talking quietly. "Hey Dandy. Think you're brave enough to come a little closer?"

Snorting warily, Dandy backed up a little.

"It's OK, boy. I know it's a big step."

Many minutes passed while Dandy contemplated his options. Then, to Vicki's surprise, he stepped forward again and nudged the apple from her hand.

It hit the ground with a plop, then the stallion dropped his head to eat it.

It was the very first time Dandy had ever touched Vicki, and a huge smile lit up her face.

"Good job," her mum said, giving her a thumbs-up. "Best to leave him now so he can think things over. That was a huge milestone for him."

Climbing down from the fence, Vicki headed to the next yard. She watched her Dad untangle a dreadlock from Squizzy's white mane.

"You're a good boy," he said, reaching forward to stroke the palamino's head. "So handsome and brave."

Unable to believe the progress her dad had made with the wild pony, Vicki watched closely, trying to learn as much as possible.

"I wonder how long it will be until Dandy will be at that stage?" she said.

Vicki watched as her dad slowly backed away from Squizzy before answering.

"I watched you with him earlier. Now that you've won his trust I think you'll be friends in no time at all."

"Really?" Vicki asked.

"I'm sure of it," her dad said. "It's taken a lot of patience to get to this point, but everything will happen a lot faster now. Just enjoy the process and let the horse pick the timing."

Vicki nodded and smiled. "I am enjoying it!

Every day I learn something new — from watching Dandy, and from seeing you and mum working with your ponies. I've learnt to stay relaxed and keep my movements slow and steady so I don't scare him."

"Good girl," her dad said. "That's the most important thing — being open to learning. I think we're all figuring it out as we go, but it seems to be working just fine."

Vicki joined Amanda and Kelly watching through the fence as their mum entered the yard to work with Jude. Although the oldest of the wild ponies, she was also coming along well.

"She's looking so good," said Vicki.

"It's only been ten days, but I'm sure her ribs are starting to disappear," Kelly replied.

"Mum said that's why they're so friendly," Amanda said as she pushed handfuls of grass through the fence to keep the foal distracted. "They're so thankful for all the grass we're picking for them."

"Look," said Kelly, pointing at Jude. "Mum's trying to halter her for the first time."

Slowly, so as not to startle the pony, Mum reached out the halter and rope, rubbing it gently against Jude's neck. Not used to the feel of the rope, Jude backed away, shaking her head. Distressed, the foal nickered and rushed to her mother's side.

Vicki watched as her mum patiently started again, slowly rubbing the horse's neck before reintroducing the rope. This time the mare stood still, although Vicki could see she was stiff with tension. Over the next twenty minutes, she slowly relaxed, until finally she stood and lowered her head into the halter and allowed it to be buckled.

With a final pat, Mum unclipped the lead rope and gave Jude's neck a rub. Smiling, she left the yard and walked over to where her family stood watching.

"Jude's haltered, Squizzy's letting Dad touch him and even Dandy is making progress," she said. "These ponies don't seem so wild anymore."

Chapter 10
Eye Level

THE NEXT DAY, DANDY MET Vicki at the fence and waited impatiently for his apple. Laughing, Vicki pulled it from her pocket and held it out for him.

"Patience," she said. "It's taken me hours to get to this point. Don't try and rush now!" Carefully he lipped it from her fingers and crunched into it.

Less than two weeks earlier he'd been all fire, but now he seemed to enjoy her visits. Holding out her hand for him to sniff, just like her parents had showed her, Vicki waited to see if Dandy would let her touch him. Stiffly, he held his head away from her. Although he hadn't taken a step back, it was obvious he wasn't ready.

Disappointed, Vicki dropped her hand. Dandy swung his head back to look at her. "What's taking you so long, huh?" Vicki asked.

Swishing his tail, Dandy yawned. Vicki's mind flashed back to the first day in the yards. He'd been so scared back then — sometimes it was hard to remember just how far he'd come.

"OK, OK, I get it," she said with a smile. "You'll trust me when you're good and ready, and not a moment before. I'm only impatient because I want to take you out of this yard so you can stretch your legs again. Wouldn't you love a gallop?"

Shaking his head, Dandy continued to watch her. His eyes were no longer wild and she could see kindness in them. She was convinced he wouldn't hurt her. She looked around to check no one was watching, then slowly climbed down the rails until she stood in the yard beside him.

"I'm not supposed to be in your yard," she whispered. "But I just want to show you how little I am. Nothing to be scared of."

Snorting, Dandy backed up, unsure about having

Vicki at eye level. He circled and stood in the corner, watching her warily. The movement drew the attention of Mum, who looked over and yelled, "Vicki, get yourself out of that yard right this minute!"

Vicki quickly climbed the rails, but she had her argument ready.

"I think I'll be less scary if I'm in the yard with him. I must look like a giant, always sitting above him," she called back.

"You should have asked first. It's not safe to try when no one is there to keep an eye on you. If anything went wrong there would be no one to help."

∪ ∪ ∪

The following day, Mum stood by the gate and nodded for Vicki to enter the yard again. "Go on, then. Grab a handful of grass and let's see how it goes."

Unable to believe she was finally allowed in the yard with Dandy, Vicki climbed down the rails again and took a step towards the watchful stallion.

"That's far enough," Mum called out. "Now keep your eyes lowered and hold the grass while you wait for him to make the next move."

Vicki waited for what felt like forever, her arm growing tired, but still Dandy didn't step forward. Minutes passed. Too tired to continue, she lowered her hand.

"Don't you dare quit now," her mum said sternly. "You're not leaving that yard until he relaxes."

Raising her hand again, Vicki waited. Every time her arm grew tired she'd lower it and swap the grass to the other hand. She talked to Dandy the whole time, softly pleading with him to trust her.

"I'm sure you're ready to be touched," she said. "But I can't force you. You're going to have to come a little closer."

Amanda and Kelly joined their mum at the rail.

"Why is Vicki standing there like a statue?" Amanda asked.

"She's giving Dandy time to get used to her."

"It doesn't seem to be working," Kelly yawned. "She's been there for ages."

"Hopefully he'll approach her soon," their mum said. "Can you see how he's starting to relax? Notice his back leg resting, and how he licks his lips."

Another half-hour passed before Dandy gathered his courage and took a cautious step towards Vicki. She waited, barely able to breathe and desperate not to scare him. Step by step the stallion crept forward.

When he was close enough, he stretched his neck to full length, tugging the grass from her outstretched fingers before backing up to eat.

"That was perfect," Mum said, smiling. "Let's leave him now and you can do more after school tomorrow."

∪ ∪ ∪

Vicki couldn't believe the transformation. The next day, as soon as she entered his yard, Dandy met her halfway. Instead of putting his evening grass in the blue drum, Vicki hand-fed him. This time her Dad supervised, still not trusting the once-wild stallion to be left alone with his little girl. Dandy still had a long way to go before Vicki would be allowed near him without an adult around.

Certain Dandy was ready for more, Vicki reached

out her other hand as he ate, to touch his head. Startled, the young stallion leapt back, eyeing her in surprise.

"I'm sorry, boy," she said. "I just couldn't resist. Shall we try again? I promise to be slower this time."

Holding up her hand slowly, she waited until he relaxed before gently reaching forward and rubbing him between the eyes. This time Dandy stood frozen — even his munching on the grass stilled as he stood to be touched for the first time.

"That's a good girl," Dad said quietly. "Keep your hand on him and rub circles on his forehead."

Slowly Vicki trailed her hands over his white blaze, almost as if she was in a dream. Dandy stood, relaxed and enjoying the attention. When she ran her hand down his nose he tensed, but Vicki was too distracted to notice him pin back his ears.

"Vicki," Dad's voice warned. "Stop what you're doing and slowly back away from him." Freezing, Vicki dropped her hand and retreated. Once she was at a safe distance, she turned to her dad with a questioning look.

"What did I do wrong?" she asked.

"You missed the warning signs," he said. "Every

time you're working with him you need to be watching his body language and the expression in his eyes. Dandy wasn't comfortable when you moved your hand down his nose. You're lucky he didn't bite your head off."

"I promise I'll pay better attention next time," Vicki said sorrowfully. "I didn't mean to upset him."

Dandy now stood relaxed.

"Now quietly try again," said Dad. "And don't let your mind wander this time. You need to be giving that pony one hundred per cent of your attention."

Chapter 11
Venturing Out

EVERY DAY THAT WEEK Vicki worked with Dandy, until she could touch him on both sides of his neck and head. Soon he was ready to be haltered.

Carefully she mimicked how she'd seen her mum catch Jude for the first time. She slowly rubbed the halter all over his neck and head before holding it in front of him to lower his muzzle into. When Dandy didn't even flinch, Vicki was elated.

"Feels weird, doesn't it?" Vicki said, patting him. "I can't believe how far you've come. Only three weeks ago you were running in the mountains, and now you trust me completely."

Dandy yawned and nudged her. "First time wearing a halter and you're already bored, huh?" said Vicki, laughing.

Turning away from her pony, Vicki glanced at her mum, patiently watching from the fence. "Can I take Dandy out for a walk? I think he's ready," she said.

"Practise leading him around the yard first," her mum replied. "Once he can turn and stop we'll open the gate and practise in the laneway."

"And if that goes well, can I take him out to the paddock so he can nibble on some fresh grass?" Vicki asked, with a hopeful smile.

"We'll see. It's taken you a lot of patience to come this far — there's no point rushing things now."

Turning back to Dandy, Vicki talked quietly to him.

"It's pretty simple, really. When I walk, you walk, and when I stop, you stop. Shall we try it?"

Stepping away, Vicki loosened the lead rope so Dandy could follow. As he was now used to being with her, he quickly mimicked her movements.

When they reached the end of the yard, Vicki

turned and continued in a circle, and again Dandy followed her lead. When she stopped, Dandy stopped beside her, and Vicki gave him a pat.

"That was perfect! Good boy!"

Looking over at her mum, Vicki raised an eyebrow in question, then smiled when she saw her mum lean over and unlatch the gate.

"He's only following you because he wants to be with you, not because he understands he's supposed to stay with you," her mum said. "Not once did you have any pressure on the rope. Be careful out there, as he won't know what it means the first time you need to tug on the halter."

When they reached the gate Dandy paused, uncertain. With a gentle but firm hold on the rope, Vicki asked him to step forward. Unsettled by the feel of the rope pulling on the halter, Dandy tossed his head and backed up. Again Vicki tugged on the lead rope and this time Dandy reared, pulling her off balance. She slipped in the mud and fell to the ground. Dandy leapt backwards in fright.

"Woah, boy," she said as she regained her footing, wiping clumps of mud off her face. "It's going to be OK."

Once Dandy relaxed again, Vicki walked up and patted his head in reassurance. Confident he was ready to try again, she walked towards the gate. This time Dandy stuck close beside Vicki, but as they stepped into the laneway he rushed forward.

Unable to hold him, Vicki dropped the lead rope. Dandy panicked as the rope snaked along behind him. Sliding into the gates at the far end, he stood, shaking.

Vicki slowly approached him. "I am so sorry," she whispered. "It shouldn't have been scary. I was only trying to give you an adventure."

Over the next half-hour, Vicki walked Dandy up and down the laneway. Once he could turn and stop, Vicki put him back in his yard and joined her mum on the fence.

"You were right," Vicki sighed. "He's not ready to go out in the paddock yet."

"It's a lot to learn for a wild horse," her mum said. "Getting used to fences, being touched by humans, and now wearing a halter and being led."

"I think we're both been learning a lot," Vicki said as she watched Dandy in his yard. "Working with him is totally different to every other pony

I've ever had."

"You've done a good job with him," her mum said. "Let's round up your dad and sister to go and cut their evening grass. I'd like to get home before dark tonight."

U U U

Two days later, after another practice in the laneway, Dandy was ready to be led out to the paddock. Vicki was careful to take things slowly, but as soon as he stepped onto the driveway he tugged on the lead, a spring in his step.

"It's a big wide world out here," said Vicki, as she struggled to keep up. "There's all sorts of things to see."

When they reached the paddock gate, she held firmly on the rope to ask Dandy to stand, and breathed a sigh of relief when he paused beside her. "Good boy!"

As soon as her mum had the gate open, Vicki led Dandy into the paddock, careful to turn him to face the gate while it was shut again so he didn't get a fright. Here the fences were wire instead of wood, and much lower than in the stockyards. Vicki hoped he wouldn't get loose and jump out.

"No silly stuff," she said sternly. "We're just out here so you can graze."

Dandy wasn't interested in the grass, though — he wanted to explore. Deciding the practice would be good for him, Vicki stepped out in front, asking him to follow. Carefully, she led him between trees and over to a little stream that ran through the paddock. When they reached the water's edge Dandy pawed at it, sending droplets flying.

"You got me wet!" Vicki said with a shriek.

She watched in surprise as Dandy buckled at the knees, laying down in the cold water to roll. Over and over he rolled, until every part of him was dripping wet. Vicki had never seen a pony roll in water before and she wondered if he'd liked to cool off in the mountain rivers when he ran wild. Tugging gently on the rope, Vicki got Dandy to stand and led him over to a weeping willow tree. This time when she stopped, he lowered his head to eat.

Chapter 12
Coming Home

By now it was the start of winter, and everyone was desperate to get the ponies out of the yards and back home. A storm was on its way, and since the stockyards had no shelter from the worsening weather, and all three ponies were now able to be safely led, the family made a plan to bring the horses home so they could be turned out into the paddocks.

On Saturday morning, Vicki and Kelly rode Twinkle and Charlie over to keep Dandy company while Squizzy and Jude were led home across the farm, leaving the foal loose to follow. The girls had ridden over a number of times now to visit the horses in the stockyards, and Dandy no longer tried to attack the other ponies — in fact, they'd almost become friends.

That afternoon they returned to the yards, this time with Dad driving the horse truck. Dandy would be led over the farm like the others, but they needed the truck for all the blue drums, the mucking-out rakes and the wheelbarrow.

As Dandy had been out of the yards only twice, Vicki was anxious about having him out in the open — but she was still disappointed when her parents decided it was safer for Mum to lead him.

"If anything goes wrong, I'll have a better chance of holding him," she said. "Especially once we get to the road, where there will be no fences to contain him if he gets loose."

"But he trusts me," Vicki argued. "I'm the only one that's worked with him."

"If we had another week to train him, it would be different. But with a storm coming, it'd be awful for him to be left shivering in these yards."

Vicki walked into Dandy's yard and quietly haltered him. Once he was caught she waited for her mum to approach. Unsure about having a stranger so close, Dandy nervously swished his tail and backed up a step.

"It's not going to work," Vicki said adamantly.

"Give him time. He's probably unsettled by having two people in his yard. You've always worked him alone. Why don't you wait by the gate while I make friends with him?" Mum replied.

Sulking, Vicki walked off and watched as her mum held out a hand to Dandy. She was torn, half hoping that she had a special bond with Dandy and that he'd ignore her mum. The other half hoped he'd be perfect so they could get him home as quickly as possible.

When Dandy stepped forward and let her mum touch him, Vicki was proud of her pony. She'd spent hours developing his trust of people and it was rewarding seeing how good he was, although she still wished she could have been the one to lead him home.

As they made their way down the laneway, Mum kept a firm grip on the lead rope. Dandy pranced beside her, tugging on the lead, excited by all the new sights. When a rabbit darted out from the hedge he startled, leaping in the air before rearing and striking out. Talking to him quietly, they waited for him to calm down before they continued.

Vicki, who was leading Charlie in front, walked backwards so she could keep an eye on Dandy. She was relieved to see him walking calmly now, occasionally bending his head to snatch mouthfuls of grass.

They walked through paddock after paddock and finally they came to the last gate. Now all that lay ahead was an old wooden bridge before they had to make their way along the road, past some houses and down the long driveway to the paddocks.

When they got to the bridge, Dandy didn't even hesitate, boldly stepping forward. Even the asphalt surface of the road didn't seem to bother him.

Soon he was safely in the front paddock, which overlooked the vegetable garden and the aviary beside the house. Setting him free with Charlie for company, Vicki watched anxiously as the ponies circled the paddock at a canter. It was the first time Dandy had been able to move that fast since he'd been running free on the mountain.

"Do you think they'll be all right together?" Vicki asked. "He won't fight Charlie, like he used to fight the other ponies in the mountains?"

"We'll watch and see," her mum said. "Hopefully not. It will be good for him to have a friend."

Soon the ponies settled down to eat, grazing side by side like old friends. It had been less than a month since Dandy had been caught, but already he looked so different. His once shiny coat was now hairy in preparation for a cold winter, and his halter, which they'd left on to make catching him easier, made him look far from wild.

"Do you think he's enjoying his life with us?" Vicki asked.

"The scariest changes are already behind him, and he's coped really well so far," Mum said, giving her a smile. "Now leave him to settle. Go find your sisters and spend some time with all your other animals, which you've been neglecting ever since these ponies came into our lives!"

Chapter 13
Stormy Weather

As THE WEEKS PASSED the weather continued to worsen, and the family could only work the wild ponies occasionally. Torrential rain had quickly turned the paddocks to mud, so once again Vicki and her sisters found themselves having to cut grass so the horses would have enough to eat.

"The rain's not going away," said Mum as they huddled inside one stormy day. "I'm worried about Dandy. He's the only pony on the property that isn't wearing a cover, and there aren't many trees for him to shelter under like he used to do on the mountain."

With a slight shiver, Vicki got up and looked out the window at the ponies. Her eyes were drawn to the chestnut, who stood huddled beside his grey companion. Both were standing with their tails to the wind.

"Do we have any covers that would fit him?" Vicki asked.

"There'll be one in the shed somewhere, but I can't imagine he's ready to wear one yet," her mother replied.

Turning away from the window, Vicki reached for her jacket. "Come on," she said, heading for the door. "Together we might be able to get him covered. It's worth a try."

Within seconds Vicki and her mum were soaked through to the skin, their coats doing little to protect them from the storm. With lowered heads they fought the wind, struggling to stay upright as they made their way to the shed.

While her mum sorted through the dusty pile of old covers, Vicki ducked back outside. "I'll be back in a second," she said. "I'm just going to feed the birds and animals since I'm already wet."

"No worries. I'll meet you at Dandy's paddock."

Avoiding the puddles that lined the driveway, Vicki grabbed handfuls of grass as she made her way along the cobbled path which led to the aviary. Her cold fingers struggled to unbolt the gate and she rubbed them together briskly to warm them.

Vicki was relieved to find the rabbits and guinea pigs in the covered part of the aviary, warm in their boxes, while above them the birds perched on branches. After tossing the animals the grass she'd picked, she checked to make sure the bird feeders were full of seeds.

"I hope the aviary doesn't flood," Vicki panted when she reached her mum, who was waiting at the hill paddock where Dandy and Charlie grazed.

Grabbing a halter from beside the gate, Vicki entered the paddock and called out for Dandy. It didn't look like he wanted to be caught, though — when he saw Vicki he took off at a gallop. The storm had obviously brought out his wild side. Vicki watched in despair as he circled the paddock, his hooves slipping and sliding in the slick mud.

"The weather has really put them on edge," her mum called out. "Wait there while I run down and get a bucket of feed."

With some carrots to tempt him, Dandy soon came close enough to be caught. Vicki kept a firm hold of his rope while her mum held out the cover. Snorting, Dandy backed up, and it took all of Vicki's strength to hold him.

"Settle down, Dandy," she said firmly. "Don't you want to be snug as a bug, in a warm woollen rug?"

Gradually he seemed to accept the feel of the cover. Although tense, Dandy stood still as it was laid over him.

"Keep a good eye on him while I do up the back straps," her mum said, reaching back to thread the leather between his hind legs. Uncomfortable, Dandy raised a leg and kicked out, narrowly missing Mum.

"It's a big ask, isn't it, boy?" Vicki said softly, as she rubbed his forehead. "You have to try a little harder, though — we're only out here in the pouring rain so you can stay dry, but if you make it too difficult we'll have to give up."

Finally the cover was secured in place. Vicki watched as her mum stuffed handfuls of hay between the cover and his back.

"What's that for?" Vicki asked.

"It will increase airflow and let his coat dry out under the cover," her mum explained.

Unclipping Dandy's rope, Vicki gave his neck a rub before turning to follow her mum to the gate. She hated to think of him being cold and miserable out in the wet weather. He was fast becoming her best friend.

Chapter 14
The Horse-Breaker

As THE WINTER PROGRESSED, the family began the task of preparing the wild ponies to be ridden. Vicki watched while her parents stood by Jude and Squizzy's shoulders, patting them on both sides of their bodies. Once the horses were comfortable with this, her parents jumped up and down beside the ponies, then sprung up and lay over their backs. The first time, the ponies stumbled from the feel of the unfamiliar weight, but they soon stood solid as her mum sat upright on Jude, and Dad walked Squizzy bareback for the first time.

Dandy, too, was ready for more, but he still wasn't very fond of having two people close to him, and he was too tall for Vicki to jump on by herself. A few times she'd tried to leap off a log or water trough onto his back, but each time Dandy leapt forward in fright and kicked out with a hind leg. Vicki was disheartened when her parents decided it wasn't safe for her to continue.

After her parents tried to work with Dandy themselves with no luck, her dad sighed. "I think it's best if we send him away to be trained by a professional."

"But he trusts me!" Vicki cried. "I just need more time."

"He's too difficult for even Dad and me to attempt to ride," her mum said. "If we don't sort this out now, he'll never be suitable for you. I saw an advertisement in the local saddlery for a guy who breaks in horses, and he's not too expensive."

"How will you afford it?" Vicki asked, secretly hoping they wouldn't have the money.

"Jude's foal is old enough to wean, so we thought we'd advertise her for sale."

Vicki was distraught. So far she'd done everything

with Dandy, and she hated the idea of someone else working with him. But nothing could change her parents' minds. The following day they advertised Jude's filly in the local paper for three hundred dollars, and organised for the horse-breaker to take Dandy.

The phone didn't stop ringing, and the first person who came to view the filly fell in love with her and bought her. Amanda was very upset when the new owners came to take her away, but she tried to put on a brave face.

"I'll miss my friend," she said tearfully, as the new owners drove off.

"I know you will," her dad said. "But this was always the plan. You have Charlie, Kelly has Twinkle, and by training and selling our two palominos we're making it possible for Vicki and mum to have their own ponies too."

"Will you miss Squizzy when he has to go?" Amanda asked, watching the trailer disappear from sight.

"Of course I will," he said. "But it's a little easier for me because he's too small for me to ride long-term. Right from the beginning I've known he'd have to go to a child one day."

♘ ♘ ♘

A few days later it was Vicki's birthday, and she woke up nervous and excited. Her parents had organised to visit the horse-breaker's property so she could watch Dandy being worked. Dandy had only been gone for a few days but already she missed him terribly.

Quickly throwing on her clothes, she rushed into the kitchen for breakfast.

"Happy birthday!" Kelly and Amanda yelled as they jumped at her, demanding a hug. "Can she open her presents now?"

From behind their backs, her parents pulled out a number of presents wrapped in newspaper. Delighted, Vicki opened them one at a time, revealing a collection of second-hand horse books.

Vicki looked up at her parents, "I love them all, thanks so much! Once we get home from seeing Dandy I'll spend the whole afternoon reading."

Hopefully you haven't read them before," grinned Mum.

"They're perfect — I'll treasure every one," said

Vicki as she carefully set aside the books.

"There's one more," Dad said, as he passed her the last present. Unlike the others, it was wrapped in gift paper, not newspaper. Knowing it must be important, Vicki carefully unwrapped it, making sure she didn't rip the paper so they could reuse it.

"Thank you, thank you!" Vicki gasped, her eyes wide as she held out a red-and-yellow rope halter and a long matching rope, with leather plaited at the end.

"The colour of fire, for your volcano pony," her dad said, smiling. "I spent hours with an old horseman I met in town, learning how to tie special knots and splice ropes. It's what you're supposed to use to tame wild horses with, not the webbing halters we've been using."

"You have no idea how much this means to me," Vicki said, as she clutched it to her chest.

∪ ∪ ∪

After lunch, they headed to the horse-breaker's property to visit Dandy. Hoping to try her new rope halter on him, Vicki laid it carefully on her lap. She was excited to see if the colours suited Dandy.

When they arrived, Dandy was already caught and the man was working him in a yard. Vicki hurried over to the rail to watch. But anger quickly spread through her as she saw Dandy fighting the rope, the kindness gone from his eyes. Bringing a whip crashing down onto his rump, the man swore.

"He's a wild one. You've got to break his spirit if you want any chance of riding him."

"Dad, he's hurting him!" Vicki yelled. Hurrying over, her father joined her at the fence, his face creasing into a frown.

"He's mean-spirited," the horse-breaker replied gruffly. "He's done nothing but try to kick and bite me since he arrived." With a jerk, the man spun Dandy around and used the whip to send him bolting in the other direction.

"Dad, you have to stop him!" Vicki cried.

Vicki's dad called the horse-breaker over to the fence line. While they talked, Vicki rushed into the yard to console her distraught pony.

"Woah, boy," she whispered as she patted his sweaty neck. "No one's going to hurt you again."

Vicki's mum pulled the car keys from her pocket.

"I'll head home and get the horse truck," she said grimly as she watched the tears streaming down her daughter's face. "He can't stay here."

∪ ∪ ∪

Before long, Dandy was safely back in his paddock at home, although he was still highly stressed.

"Mum, no matter how long it takes, promise you'll let me train him," Vicki demanded. "We can't let him go through that again."

Her mum shook her head sadly. "You know I can't do that. My number-one priority is to keep you safe, and if he's too difficult I'm not going to let you be the first to ride him."

"Then I'll wait a year — or more. I'm willing to take as long as he needs."

"We'll see how it goes," Mum replied. "He'll need plenty of love from you over the next few weeks though, that's for sure." She looked Vicki in the eye. "You know we never intended for him to be trained that way, right?"

"I know that," Vicki replied, dejected. Scuffing her boot in the dirt, she whispered, "I just feel so guilty. I taught Dandy to trust humans and now he's been hurt because of it."

Chapter 15
Lost Trust

VICKI STRUGGLED TO WIN BACK Dandy's trust. Every time she raised a hand to pat him, he would cower in fear. It was even worse if her dad was in sight — Dandy would start trembling as soon as he heard a man's voice.

"I'm so sorry, boy," said Vicki. "No matter how long it takes, or how patient I have to be, I'll make sure you're trained with kindness."

It took quite a few weeks, but by September Dandy was almost back to his old self, and Vicki was once again starting to see progress. She could now bridle and saddle him, and once he was geared up she would lead him around the farm behind Charlie.

One day, when they were visiting the saddlery, her mum pointed out a poster for a Colt Starting clinic with a Natural Horsemanship trainer. People could bring along young horses and learn how to train them themselves, under supervision.

"Vicki, should we see if there's a space available? It might be just what we need to get Dandy ready to be ridden. This way you can be involved in the process."

Vicki looked at the poster. "'Gentling' horses sounds much nicer than the horse-breaker's way of training Dandy! I'm sure he's ready to try again, and he'll be more relaxed if I'm the one riding him."

"Don't get ahead of yourself, young lady," her mum said, laughing. "There's still a month until the clinic, and then we'll let the expert decide if Dandy's ready for you to ride."

"I'll spend lots of time with him before then, getting him ready," Vicki promised.

U U U

Vicki spent all her spare time with Dandy, preparing for the clinic, and reading as much as she could about horse training. On the weekends, the whole family would head out on the farm, with everyone else riding while Vicki walked behind, leading Dandy.

The night before the clinic, Vicki washed Dandy, picked out his hooves and covered him so he'd stay clean. The next morning, they drove to the rodeo grounds. Once Dandy was unloaded, she groomed him to perfection, using a curry comb to loosen his winter coat. He was starting to look glossy again. No one looking at him now would have known that he'd roamed wild just five months earlier.

Eleven other horses were at the clinic. Over the course of the day Vicki and her mum learnt a lot about horses' natural instincts and body language, working Dandy through different exercises. Although he was still hesitant around some men, Dandy didn't seem to mind the natural horsemanship trainer.

"I think he knows you're trying to make things easier for him," Vicki said, when the trainer came over to show her when to hold and when to release the pressure on the rope.

"It's about communicating with our horses in a way they understand," he said. "Timing is so important, because we want our horses to be soft and responsive."

"He's starting to get it," said Vicki, as she asked Dandy to work through the exercise again. "Thanks for showing me. I'm learning a lot."

"You'd have to be the youngest rider I've ever had at my clinics," the trainer said, as he watched on. "You've got a great feel for horses."

"Do you think he'll be ready for me to ride soon?" Vicki asked hesitantly. 'Every time I try to jump on him he leaps sideways and I end up on the ground."

"If I think he's ready, we can try tomorrow. Otherwise, I could work with him for a couple of weeks and get him ready for you to ride."

Nervously, Vicki twisted the rope between her hands.

"We sent Dandy to a horse-breaker a few months ago and he got mistreated," she said. "I promised him I wouldn't send him away again."

"You know what's best for your pony," the trainer

said, as he reached out to pat Dandy's head. "But if you need a little help, I'd be more than happy to work with him. I think he's very trainable, and with a little patience and a gentle touch, he'd be going kindly under saddle in no time at all."

U U U

The next day Vicki and Dandy continued to make progress, but the trainer still didn't think he was ready for more.

"There's a lot of distractions here, and it's better not to rush a first ride," he said. "We want it to be a fun and positive experience for him."

After having stayed up most of the night before thinking about Dandy's future, Vicki had made a decision about what he needed.

She told the trainer, "Mum and I talked about it, and we would like you to train him — on one condition. We would like to come and watch on the weekends when you're working with him."

"I'd be happy with that," the trainer agreed. "I'll talk you through everything, step by step, and maybe you'll learn a thing or two."

"I'd love that," said Vicki.

That afternoon, once the clinic was finished, Vicki loaded Dandy onto the trainer's horse truck. They would collect him in two weeks' time. The trainer normally spent six weeks starting young horses under saddle, but as her mum and dad couldn't afford that much time he was willing to make an exception.

Although Vicki was nervous sending Dandy away again, this time she was confident he'd feel safe at the trainer's property. She was looking forward to visiting him at the weekend to see his progress.

∪ ∪ ∪

The school week seemed to drag on forever. Vicki was desperate to check on Dandy and make sure he was happy, and equally excited to see how much he'd learnt in the six days he'd been gone.

The drive north to the trainer's property took over an hour. Vicki fidgeted in the back seat, annoying her sisters.

"How long to go?" Vicki asked for the millionth time.

"Two minutes less than the last time you asked," Kelly muttered.

"Girls, stop it," their mum said. "We're not far away now."

After what seemed like hours, they pulled into the driveway. As soon as the car was parked, Vicki jumped out and rushed over to where the trainer was waiting for them.

"How's he been going?" Vicki asked in a rush.

Reaching for a halter, he replied, "Why don't you follow me and see for yourself?"

Falling into step behind him, Vicki walked over to the paddock where Dandy grazed. To Vicki's relief, Dandy appeared settled. When he saw the trainer at the gate, he walked up to be caught without a moment's hesitation.

"He seems to trust you," Vicki said.

"He's been trying really hard this past week. You should be very proud of him."

Pleased, Vicki watched as the trainer groomed Dandy before leading him over to the round-shaped yard. For the next fifteen minutes Vicki watched him doing groundwork with Dandy, listening closely as the trainer talked through what he was doing and why.

Satisfied with how Dandy was working, the trainer brought the pony into the centre of the yard and stood quietly beside his shoulder. Unable to believe her eyes, Vicki watched as he leapt up onto Dandy's back, riding him without a saddle.

Although he flicked an ear, Dandy didn't move, and stood waiting quietly for direction. With a soft cluck, the trainer urged him forward. Slowly, Dandy circled the yard. With a slight squeeze on the rope from his rider, Dandy came to a crooked halt in front of his audience, and the trainer dismounted.

"At times he's slightly wobbly and unsure of what's being asked of him, but he's come a long way," he said.

"He looks amazing!" gushed Vicki. "Thank you so much!"

The trainer gave Dandy's neck a gentle pat.

"He'll be ready for you in no time. I'll hopefully get our first trot and canter over the next few days, then I'll give you a lesson when you collect him next weekend."

Speechless, Vicki nodded frantically, unable to believe she'd finally be able to ride Dandy. She'd waited for this moment for over six months.

Entering the yard, she slid her arms around Dandy's neck and gave him a hug.

"Did you hear that, boy? It's going to be the first of many adventures!" As if he understood her, Dandy nudged her with his head, and Vicki laughed.

Chapter 16
First Ride … and a Fall

THE NEXT WEEK SEEMED TO crawl by, but eventually it was the morning of Vicki's big ride. From the moment she woke up she was filled with anticipation. Impatient to see Dandy, she hurried everyone through breakfast.

Again, the car trip seemed to take forever. She talked non-stop, her excitement driving everyone else crazy. It wasn't until they pulled into the driveway that she finally stopped talking and her family breathed a sigh of relief.

Just like their last visit, Vicki watched while the

trainer put Dandy through his paces, riding him bareback. He'd improved so much in a week! No longer confused, Dandy strode out well, stopping and turning when asked.

As he rode, the trainer talked Vicki through the cues Dandy now understood, so he would know when she wanted him to start, stop or turn. Vicki carefully took note — she didn't want to forget a thing. She watched in awe as they trotted then

cantered around the yard, before the trainer brought Dandy back to a walk and rode over to the gate.

"Are you ready to ride?" he asked. "It'll have to be bareback, though, as he's only had the saddle on a few times so far."

Vicki nodded her head, fumbling as she tried to open the gate. "That's OK — I ride bareback at home all the time."

"Come on over then, he's all ready for you," he said.

Holding Dandy steady, the trainer leant over and gave Vicki a leg up. She could hardly believe she was riding Dandy for the very first time, when just a few weeks earlier she'd doubted it would ever be possible. From the rails, her parents and sisters watched as she gathered the rope reins, everyone beaming from ear to ear.

"Very carefully, you're going to open the outside rein and ask him to go forward by gently squeezing your legs," the trainer instructed. "We want him working around the outside of the round yard."

Careful to follow his instructions, Vicki guided Dandy around the pen, making sure to stay relaxed so Dandy wouldn't become tense.

"You're doing an amazing job, Dandy," she said,

reaching forward to pat him.

"You're not doing too bad yourself," the trainer said. "Ready for a trot?"

With a click of her tongue, she squeezed her legs to ask for a trot and Dandy increased his stride. His paces were smooth and effortless.

"Good job, Vicki. Squeeze him on a little more and let's see if he'll canter for you."

As Vicki urged him forward again, Dandy changed into the three-beat gait. Beneath her, she could hear the pounding of his hooves. She glanced down at his pricked ears and his mane flowing in the wind. It was a magical first ride, and when they came back to a halt she couldn't stop smiling. Riding her wild mountain pony was everything she'd dreamed of.

"That was the best feeling ever!" said Vicki, her heart in her mouth. "Thank you so much for training him!"

"Oh, I didn't do too much," the trainer said. "You did most of the hard work, winning his trust over the past six months."

Not wanting to dismount, Vicki stayed on Dandy while the trainer talked with her parents, patting

Dandy for being such a good boy. But all too soon it was time to leave. Vicki swung off him.

"Ready to come home?" she asked Dandy. "I bet you missed all your friends."

With a snort, Dandy nuzzled Vicki's neck.

∪ ∪ ∪

Back at home later that afternoon, Vicki was helping her sisters feed the birds and animals in the aviary when Kelly said wistfully, "You are so lucky to be able to ride Dandy — he's so beautiful."

"I'll let you ride him if you want," Vicki replied.

"Really?" said Kelly, jumping up and down in excitement. "Can I ride him now?"

Vicki hesitated. She hadn't meant today, but seeing how excited Kelly was she felt mean saying no.

"OK then, but just bareback and only on the lead rein."

Heading to the paddock, Vicki caught Dandy and led him over to where Kelly and Amanda stood waiting by the gate.

"Come over here and I'll help you get on," Vicki said.

Holding up a leg, Kelly waited for Vicki to give her a boost. Dandy was much higher than her pony Twinkle, and as she jumped up she clutched his mane, trying to wriggle her way onto his back.

Startled, Dandy leapt in the air, and Kelly lost her balance and slipped off. Dandy kicked out in fright, but this time he didn't miss. With a sickening thud, he double-barrelled Kelly, both of his hind hooves connecting with her knees.

Kelly crashed to the ground and lay where she'd fallen, screaming in agony. The noise brought Amanda and their parents running, and they rushed to Kelly's side. Relieved, Vicki headed over to reassure Dandy before returning to watch her parents check Kelly over.

"Your knees are already swollen and bruising," Mum said as she carefully rolled up Kelly's pants. "He must have hit you hard — I can see hoof marks!"

"It hurts so much," Kelly whimpered.

"Let's get you to bed," Mum said, gathering Kelly in her arms. "I don't think anything's broken, but you won't be walking for a few days."

Dad turned to Vicki. "You can't leave him like that, you know — you'll have to ride him now, so he finishes up on a good note."

Feeling terrible, Vicki nodded. "I hope Kelly will be OK"

"I can't believe you thought it was a good idea to let your sister ride him. What were you thinking?" her dad said sternly.

Already feeling bad, Vicki mumbled an apology and quietly set to work with Dandy. Once he was ready to mount, her dad came over to help. This time Dandy stood quietly while Vicki was legged up onto his back.

As he had been on her ride that morning at the trainer's, Dandy was well-behaved, and Vicki walked and trotted him for a few minutes before dismounting. He'd had a big day and she didn't want to tire him out.

"No more pony rides for this wild thing," her dad said. "As soon as Dandy's settled in his paddock you need to come to the house and make sure Kelly is OK. She'll be hurting pretty badly, so you will have to do all her chores until she's feeling better."

Feeling thoroughly chastened, Vicki headed up

the hill with Dandy. She'd been kicked by a pony once and had limped for days, so she could only imagine how sore Kelly would be with both knees injured. She was just thankful that Dandy would still let her get on his back.

Chapter 17
New Experiences

WEEKS PASSED, AND WITH every ride Vicki and Dandy's bond grew stronger. Soon they were riding out on the hills with the other horses. First Dandy was ridden bareback, then he progressed to being ridden with a saddle and bridle.

However, the palamino stallion still had to be sold. By early December Squizzy was ready to be advertised, and, just like when his golden daughter went up for sale, the phone didn't stop ringing.

Out of all the people who came to look him over, Dad felt the best home for Squizzy might be with a fourteen-year-old girl who was very confident at working with young ponies. Her family owned a farm, and they all rode — it sounded like the perfect home.

When they arrived, Vicki caught Squizzy and saddled him, before riding him so they could see how he worked. Impressed, the girl rode him next. She soon fell in love with his golden colouring, sweet temperament and dependable nature.

"I absolutely love him," she said, as she swung from the saddle and hugged him. "I've looked at a lot of ponies and he's the best by far."

Determined not to miss out, the girl and her parents returned later that day to pay for him, with their horse trailer in tow so they could take him home. Everyone was sad to see Squizzy leave.

"I'm going to miss that pony," Dad said sadly.

The sale of Squizzy brought in more than enough money to pay the bills, which had been building up while the three wild ponies were being worked with. The remaining money was put into a special new account, which would be the start of a nest egg for when they needed to buy bigger ponies for Kelly and Amanda, or for new riding gear as they outgrew their old things.

With Squizzy gone, Dad had more spare time in the evenings. To keep busy, he dragged a few logs out of the river for Vicki to teach Dandy to jump over.

"We'll have him ready for shows in no time," he said at dinner that night.

"You really think so?" Vicki asked.

"Let's take him to Pony Club next week and see

how he copes," her mum said. "If that goes well, you could aim for the local Ribbon Day next month."

U U U

It had been about eight months since Vicki, Kelly and Amanda had last attended Pony Club, back when they still had Cardiff, and they were excited by the prospect of catching up with all their riding friends and entering a show. It had been hard work over winter, with the wild ponies needing so much attention.

Because it was Dandy's first rally, Vicki was unsure how he would go. "He's never jumped over coloured poles before, and I'm not sure how he'll cope with the other ponies, either," she told the instructor.

"No worries," the instructor said. "We'll take it slowly."

They warmed up slowly, focusing on their transitions between paces: walk, trot, walk, halt, trot, canter, walk.

"It's pretty complicated, isn't it, Dandy?" Vicki

said, as he shook his head in confusion.

At home they'd mostly been riding out on the farm, so the flat work was good practice for Dandy. He'd need to be confident working in a big circle with lots of other ponies if they wanted to compete at the upcoming Ribbon Day.

Once they began jumping, Dandy was still a little unsure, spooking in front of the scarier fences. Vicki was relieved the jumps were small enough for Dandy to clear, even if he hesitated and had to jump from a standstill. Each time they landed, Vicki gave him a pat so he knew he'd been good, and the second time around he jumped them perfectly, boldly cantering into the jumps.

Dandy's next round was even better, and he kept a consistent rhythm as he made his way around the jumps. "That was good, Vicki," the instructor called out. "Excellent job getting him around that course. You can finish with that — it's a good note to end on." Once Vicki finished, the instructor raised the fences to 60 centimetres for the other riders. Vicki watched as Kelly jumped Twinkle around the course clear.

As they drove home late that evening, the three

sisters chatted away, talking about the highlights of their day. They couldn't wait to return to Pony Club the following week.

"Dandy was amazing!" Vicki said proudly. "I'm sure he'll be ready for the Ribbon Day in three weeks."

Chapter 18
Ribbon Day

THE MORNING OF THE RIBBON DAY dawned clear, and Vicki and her sisters woke at 6 a.m. to groom and plait their ponies' manes and tails. Unlike when she'd ridden Cardiff, Vicki wasn't expecting lots of ribbons — she was just excited to get Dandy out to his first show. She wanted it to be a good experience for him, and hoped it would be the first of many.

Once the ponies were ready, Vicki, Kelly and Amanda loaded them onto their little horse truck and their parents drove them the five minutes to the showgrounds.

"I can't believe we're at our first show," Vicki said to Dandy as she unloaded him. "It's been less than a year since you were wild, and now look at you!"

Cars and trucks were everywhere and people bustled backwards and forwards. Dandy stood alert, taking everything in, while Vicki oiled his hooves and brushed out his tail. She was careful to make sure no one approached Dandy, as he was still a little unsettled around strangers and she didn't want him upset before the show started.

Dandy's coat shone like copper from all the grooming. As Vicki saddled him up she couldn't help but admire him.

"I think you're the most beautiful pony in the whole world," she said. "I'm so lucky to have you."

Once he was ready, Vicki changed into her jodhpurs and Pony Club uniform, then helped Kelly and Amanda get ready. Soon they all looked identical in their matching yellow-and-black jerseys. Dashing outside, they pulled on their helmets and bridled their waiting ponies.

Finally, it was time for the show to start. Vicki led Dandy over to the ring.

As they waited by the gate to go in, one of the

other ponies snaked its head at Dandy, trying to bite him. On instinct, Dandy reared up, striking out with his hooves, and the other ponies scattered.

"Woah, boy, calm down," said Vicki, firmly tugging on the reins.

Above the chaos, Vicki heard a snarky comment from one of the girls waiting to compete.

"Those sisters always have the most feral horses," she said, her nose in the air.

"And their gear is always so old," her friend replied. "I'd be too embarrassed to be seen in public if I looked like that."

Turning away, Vicki brought her focus back to Dandy, careful to keep him relaxed. "You might have been wild once, but you're certainly not feral," she whispered to him. "We'll just have to prove them wrong, won't we?"

When the judge finally called them into the ring for the Best Groomed category, Vicki was careful to keep Dandy beside Twinkle so he wouldn't get stressed by the other ponies. The fire in his eyes had long subsided, however, and he stood calmly waiting for the judge to walk down the line.

All the hours of grooming paid off, and Vicki was

thrilled to place third in the class. It was Dandy's first ribbon! The next class was Rider on the Flat, Ten Years and Under.

"I can't wait till you're eleven. It not fair that I have to compete against you!" Kelly complained.

Vicki laughed. "I think you'll have plenty of chance to beat me today, since it's Dandy's first show," she told her sister.

A hopeful gleam entered Kelly's eyes and she urged Twinkle into the ring.

Judging soon began, and everything was going well until the judge asked everyone to canter. A pony rushed up behind Dandy and he got a fright, tossing his neck as he leapt in the air. Unbalanced, Vicki lost her stirrup and it took all of her strength to stay on.

"It's OK, boy," Vicki said as she shortened her reins and steadied him. Soon Dandy was settled and they continued on, changing pace and direction before the judge called the winners into the centre.

"First place is number thirty-nine."

Vicki continued trotting, waiting for the judge to call out the next placegetters before dismissing the other riders. "Can I please have number thirty-nine, the chestnut," the judge repeated.

Looking around, Vicki saw the judge waving her arm to call her in. Her jaw dropped in surprise. She'd won the class!

Asking Dandy back to a walk, she approached the judge and lined up for her ribbon. "Sorry," said Vicki. "I didn't think it could possibly be me."

"I thought you rode remarkably," the judge replied, smiling. "He's obviously an inexperienced pony and you weren't at all flustered when he leapt about. You have such a good seat and kind, soft hands. Well done."

Unable to contain her grin, Vicki led the other placegetters out of the ring, cantering out on a lap of honour.

In the next class, Best Paced and Mannered, Dandy didn't place. Although his paces were beautiful, his manners left much to be desired — unlike Twinkle, who placed second, much to Kelly's delight.

Next was Novice Pony, for any pony that had never won a first-place ribbon. Unlike the other classes, which each had about twenty ponies competing, there were only four novices.

Dandy worked well, and again the judge called him in, this time in second place. While she waited for the judge to announce the rest of the placings, Vicki leant forward and gave Dandy a hug. She was so proud of how well he was going. It was even better than she could have dreamed.

∪ ∪ ∪

At lunch, they headed back to the truck to eat. First, they loosened the girths on their ponies' saddles and offered them food and water. It had been a big morning for them, too. All three ponies dozed while Amanda filled in the older girls on her successes with Charlie, since she had been competing in a different ring.

"I won three red ribbons," Amanda said proudly.

"Really? That's amazing!" said Vicki. "Which classes?"

"We won Best Groomed, even though I forgot to pick out Charlie's hooves," Amanda said with a cheeky grin. "Luckily the judge didn't check!"

"There's a first time for everything," Kelly said

with a laugh. "Your pony is never the best groomed."

Poking out her tongue, Amanda continued. "I also won Rider on the Flat and Best Pony Club Mount."

"Congratulations," Vicki said. "That means you'll be in the Junior Ring next time, competing with us!"

"It hardly seems fair having to compete against you, Vicki — you're twice my age!" Amanda said, as she took a bite from her apple.

"I'm sure you'll hold your own," Kelly said.

"My plan is to beat you both," Amanda said confidently. "Charlie and I are on a winning streak."

"Good luck with that," said Vicki. "Dandy is by far the best pony I've ever owned. He'll be a champion in no time!"

Chapter 19
Leap of Faith

AFTER THE LUNCH BREAK, the girls returned to the arena for the jumping classes. This time the riders entered the ring one at a time and jumped around a course. The first class was Eye Opener, a chance for all the ponies to jump the course and have a practice.

It was lucky that this round wasn't judged, because Dandy was very spooky, hesitating at many of the jumps. Then at the brush jump, a natural obstacle filled with branches, Dandy leapt over it like it was a Grand Prix fence, and Vicki lost her balance on landing, falling to the ground.

"That hurt," Vicki said to her pony, as she gingerly rose to her feet. "The way you're jumping you'd think you were at the Horse of the Year Show. Next time remember the jumps are only 50 centimetres, so I can stay on."

Leading him from the ring, Vicki waited for the next class, hoping they'd be able to jump around clear.

The rider class was next. Vicki would be judged on her position over the fences and how well she rode, and she was relieved when the judge said they had to jump only the first three jumps. Happy she wouldn't have to jump the brush, Vicki and Dandy trotted into the ring and halted, saluting to the judge like she'd been taught to do at Pony Club.

Picking up a canter, she and Dandy approached the first upright. Safely over, they continued on to the next, before turning and jumping the last. Vicki circled and brought Dandy back to a trot, then a halt, again saluting to the judge.

"Good boy, Dandy," Vicki said proudly. "That was perfect!"

At the completion of the class, Vicki was called

into the ring as the winner, with Kelly second. As the red ribbon was tied around Vicki's arm, the judge said, "Congratulations — it's not often the same person wins both the flat and jumping rider classes. You're going to go a long way."

Moving on to Twinkle, she placed a blue ribbon on Kelly's arm. "You two are the cutest combination! Most kids your age are still on the lead rein."

"Thanks!" Kelly replied with a toothy grin. "Twinkle's the best pony."

The next class was Open Hunter. This meant jumping not only the brush, but also a wire jump, so Vicki was very nervous. They'd practised it only once at Pony Club, and Vicki wasn't sure if Dandy would jump it on his first attempt.

Knowing she would get nervous watching the other horses compete, Vicki offered to go first. She gamely cantered into the first jump. Soon they were approaching the brush, but unlike in Eye Opener, Dandy jumped it effortlessly, placing one canter stride between the two fences. Continuing on, they re-jumped the first three jumps before turning and approaching the wire.

Three strides out, Dandy hesitated and fell back

to a trot. Urging him on, Vicki kept him straight and he jumped it clear, although rather awkwardly.

"You are such a brave boy," Vicki said, as she gave him a big pat.

Although they'd lost all chance of placing because Dandy had trotted, Vicki was incredibly pleased with her pony. She waited outside the ring to see how her younger sister would fare.

Twinkle jumped around clear but fitted two canter strides in between the brushes — Twinkle's little legs just couldn't make the distance. Kelly was thrilled to place third.

"Well done," said Vicki, leaning over to pat the little grey pony. "I've never seen Twinkle jump so well!"

The last class of the day was Tip 'n' Out, a competition to see who could jump the highest. The jump started with just a pole on the ground, and each round it was raised a further 10 centimetres for the riders who jumped it clear.

Up and up the jumps went. When Dandy cleared 70 centimetres, the highest he'd ever jumped, Vicki leant forward and gave him a hug. Riding over to her mum and dad, who stood watching from the sidelines with Amanda, she asked, "Do you think I should finish? I'm really happy with him!"

Her mum shook her head. "He's jumping it so easily — why don't you keep jumping and see what he's capable of?"

"If we clear the next height, it'll be the highest I've ever jumped on any pony in my life," said Vicki.

"You've got this, kiddo. Remember to keep your legs against his sides to keep him moving forward, and look up," her dad said.

Turning around, Vicki headed back to where eight other ponies stood waiting for the jump to be raised.

"You're still in!" Vicki said when she saw Kelly waiting with Twinkle.

"Yeah, but I'm pretty scared," Kelly said with a worried look. "I've never jumped this high!"

"Me neither," said Vicki. "But if Dandy can do it after learning to jump only a couple of months ago, I'm sure Twinkle can too."

"You go before me, then."

When it was her turn, Vicki asked Dandy for a canter and approached the fence, careful to follow her dad's advice. At the base of the fence she felt

Dandy gather his legs beneath him, soaring over the pole with plenty of room to spare.

"We did it, Dandy!" Vicki cried out. "We've just beaten my personal best!"

Dropping back to a walk, Vicki turned to watch Kelly approach on Twinkle. Very gallantly they cantered towards the jump, but at the last second Twinkle darted sideways and went around it instead.

As she trotted past Vicki, Kelly flashed her a grin. "It's OK — I didn't really want to jump it anyway."

Now the jump was raised again, this time to

90 centimetres. Only three ponies remained in the competition.

"Do you think we'll be able to clear it?" she asked Dandy, as she stroked his neck. "It's pretty big."

Approaching the jump Vicki tried to keep a steady canter, but a few strides out Dandy fell back into a trot. Keeping him straight, she urged him forward again with her legs.

"Come on Dandy, you can jump it," she said as he took off. As if in slow motion Vicki felt Dandy tuck his legs, stretching as he tried to clear the jump. Before she knew it they were on the other side, clear!

"I can't believe you made it, Dandy!" she cried. "You are the best pony in the world!"

Vicki was so caught up in her conversation with Dandy that she didn't notice the other ponies drop the rail. When the judge walked towards her with the red ribbon she was shocked.

"Did we really win?" she asked in disbelief.

"You certainly did," the judge said. How long have you had your pony for?"

Quickly Vicki told her the story about how Dandy had been captured from the wild and how she'd tamed and trained him. The judge was obviously interested in the tale.

"You should be incredibly proud of your hard work," she said. "He's a lovely pony, and I'm really impressed by your riding. Just keep doing what you're doing." The judge gave Dandy an affectionate scratch behind the ear.

"Thanks so much — I love jumping and hope to be a Grand Prix showjumper one day," Vicki said, unable to contain her excitement.

Vicki cantered out of the ring, her red ribbon fluttering in the breeze. As she completed her lap of honour, she imagined she was riding a mighty show jumper at the Horse of the Year, after winning at the biggest event in the country.

With a grin, she shook her head. Now wouldn't that be something.

Squeezing her reins, she slowed Dandy and bought him back to a trot, then a walk. Riding over to her family, she couldn't stop smiling.

"Thanks for believing in me and helping me tame Dandy — it's been the best year of my life!" Vicki said to her parents.

"You deserve it, kiddo," her dad replied. "You've worked hard for it."

Dismounting, Vicki threw her arms around Dandy's neck. "From the first moment I saw you galloping in the mountains, I knew you were special."

Her mum pulled Vicki into a hug. "I have a feeling you are both destined to be champions."

Dandy

Just Fine 'n' Dandy is a real pony and this book is based on events that really happened!

Dandy is a 13.2-hand, chestnut Welsh gelding, with a blaze, three white socks and a large brown birthmark on his right hind leg. He was born in 1992 in Northland, and was mustered in 1996 when he was four years old. He lived with our family for six years, being tamed by Vicki and then ridden and competed by all three of us, before we eventually outgrew him and he went to a younger rider. He was a versatile all rounder, competing in Pony Club events, dressage formation rides, cross country, showjumping and game competitions, recording many wins. He was also awarded Supreme Champion Show Pony multiple times. You will meet Dandy's best friend, Cameo, in the next book in the *Showtym Adventures* series and find out more about his ongoing adventures!

Characters

Vicki has always shown talent for riding, training and competing with horses. She has won national titles and championships in Showing, Show Hunter and Show Jumping, and has represented New Zealand internationally. Dandy was the first pony she trained, when she was nine years old, and then 20 years later she won the World Championships for Colt Starting. When she's not riding she loves to learn as much about horses as she can, from farriers, vets, physios and dentists.

Kelly has always been creative. She loves horses, photography and writing. Although she competed to Grand Prix level when she was 16, now she only show jumps for fun, and also enjoys taming wild horses. Her favourite rides are out on the farm, swimming in the river, or cantering down the beach. When she's not on a horse, she is very daring, and loves going on extreme adventures.

Amanda is the family comedian and can always make people laugh! As a child she was always pulling pranks and getting up to mischief. Amanda began show jumping at a young age and competed in her first Grand Prix when she was 12. In 2010 she won the Pony of the Year, the most prestigious Pony Grand Prix in the Southern Hemisphere, and since then she has had lots of wins up to World Cup level. When she's not outside training her horses or teaching other riders, Amanda loves doing something creative — she has already filmed two documentaries and is writing her first book.

Mum (Heather Wilson) grew up with a love of horses, although she was the only one in her family to ride. She volunteered at a local stable from the age of 13, teaching herself to ride when she was gifted an injured racehorse. Although she only rides occasionally now, her love of horses hasn't faded over the years and she is always ringside to watch her daughters compete. In her spare time she loves painting and drawing anything to do with horses, and as 'Camp Mum' is popular with the young riders who attend Showtym Camps.

Dad (John Wilson) grew up with horses, hunting, playing polo and riding on the farm. His family also show jumped and trained steeplechasers, so he has loved horses from a young age. He hurt his back when he was in his twenties, which has limited his horse riding, but he enjoys watching his daughters ride and is very proud of their success. When he's not fixing things around the farm, he can be found gardening or creating stunning life-sized horse sculptures from recycled horseshoes.

How-tos

The most important thing about owning a pony is to learn as much as you can about their care and training, so you can make their life as fun and easy as possible! In each book in the *Showtym Adventures* series, we will expand on key lessons Vicki, Amanda and I learnt on our journey to becoming better horse riders. Some lessons we learnt by making mistakes; others from observing our horses and learning from them — and some knowledge has been passed down to us by others. We hope you enjoy these top tips!

How to tie a pony

When Vicki tied Dandy up for the first time she
made sure to use a quick release knot, like her
parents had taught her when she was a young girl.
That way if he were to panic, or get a leg caught
over the rope and pull back, Vicki would be able to
untie him quickly and safely.

Follow the diagram below to learn how to tie a quick
release knot:

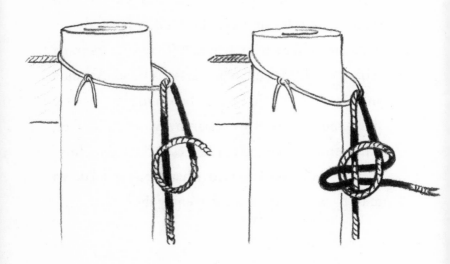

Here are some top tips from Vicki about tying up your pony:

- Tie your pony at a safe height. The rope should be tied at about the same height as your pony's back. If you tie your pony too low it can get a leg over the rope, or get its head stuck underneath the rope, and panic.
- Tie your pony at a length that's long enough for it to be comfortable, but not so long that the rope droops down — otherwise the pony will be able to step over it.
- Do not tie up your pony with the bridle. Instead, use a good quality, properly fitting halter and a lead rope.
- Only tie your pony to objects that it cannot move or pull over, like a tree trunk or a strong post. Never tie your pony to something it can drag, like a large tyre or horse trailer that's not attached to a vehicle.
- Tie your pony to a piece of twine that is tied to something sturdy. This way, if your pony pulls back to break free only the twine is broken, reducing the chance of injury to your pony.

How to use a rope halter

Rope halters can be a good tool for training your pony, allowing you to communicate quickly and precisely by applying pressure to the lead rope. If your pony pulls on the rope, the halter becomes uncomfortable. If your pony yields to the pressure, it can be rewarded instantly by softening the halter.

When Vicki first used her birthday rope halter on Dandy, she didn't realise there was a right way and a wrong way of fitting it. At the Colt Starting clinic the trainer showed her how to correctly fit the halter to Dandy's head, so the rope halter sat high up on his nose, just below the cheekbones.

He also showed her how to tie it correctly so the knot was around the loop of the halter and the end of the rope faced away from Dandy's eye.

The diagram opposite shows the correct way to fit your pony's rope halter.

TOP TIP

Rope halters should never be left on your pony in a yard or paddock. When you are not with your pony, it is important that a halter can break if it accidentally gets caught on something. Rope halters are too strong for this, so can potentially cause injury.

How to reward a pony

Ponies learn well from being rewarded. There are four main ways you can communicate to your pony when they have done something well:

1. Use your voice to praise your pony.
2. Release any pressure from your hands or legs as soon as your pony makes the tiniest effort to correctly respond to your instruction. For example, when Vicki was working with Dandy at the Colt Starting clinic, the trainer taught her to release the pressure on the rope as soon as Dandy showed any sign of stepping forward.
3. Pat or stroke your pony's head or neck.
4. Feed your pony a treat.

How to feed your pony a treat

It is important to only feed your pony treats in small portions. If you feed it treats all the time it can start to expect them and can become pushy or nippy. Horse bites hurt so make sure to hold your hand flat, with the food or treat on your palm (take a look at the drawing of Vicki feeding Dandy on page 70). This will keep your fingertips away from the pony's mouth, making it less likely for you to be bitten.

Top treat ideas:

- Grass
- Hay
- Apples (Dandy's favourite!)
- Carrots

TOP TIP

Another great treat idea is to feed your pony a small handful of its normal feed, such as pellets of chaff.

Thank you

Dandy's story is made special because he was the first wild pony we ever encountered. Our memories of him are remembered through the eyes of young children; although he was mustered from a mountain and unhandled, I'm sure he wasn't as wild as the Kaimanawas, Mustangs or Brumbies we have tamed in recent years. But to us he was the wild stallion of our dreams — just like the ones we'd read about in our favourite books. As the first pony Vicki ever trained, Dandy has taught us countless lessons, many of which stood Vicki in good stead when she won the World Championship of Colt Starting in America. So thank you Dandy for helping to define our formative years with horses!

Dandy's story, and the entire *Showtym Adventures* series, is based on true events from our childhood. First and foremost, we have to thank our parents for allowing us the opportunity to own ponies, even when it made no financial sense do to so. Every success we have had with horses has been because of their sacrifices, and we are so appreciative that they passed on their love of horses to us.

As young children we learnt that we had to work hard for what we wanted, and since we valued riding above most things, we didn't mind the hours of hard work required to keep our dreams alive. We are thankful our parents encouraged us to wholeheartedly chase our dreams, and never told us it was impossible to change our circumstances. We never heard the word 'No'; rather Mum and Dad would ask, 'How were we going to make it happen'. We developed a strong work ethic because of their support, and always looked outside the box to solve problems.

Because we couldn't afford well-trained ponies or riding lessons, most of what we learnt was from our ponies themselves — and often the hard way! Through this process of trial and error, we learnt compassion for our ponies. They were our friends and we treated them as equals.

There were many times, however, when we were ignorant and made mistakes, but we hope our ponies understood that we always had kind intentions. The past two decades have been dedicated to learning as much as possible about our four-legged partners; we know so much more now than we did at the beginning. We also realise that our current understanding will be a shadow of how much we're going to know in another 20 years!

Alongside our parents and our ponies, are my two sisters who made this book possible. We were lucky to be the best of friends growing up, always going on adventures or making mischief together. I consider myself lucky to have had such a rough-and-tumble childhood, and I hope that one day my own kids can enjoy the same kind of adventures as we had in the great outdoors.

Lastly, thank you to the thousands of young riders we have had the privilege to teach over the past 12 years. To every rider that has attended our Showtym Camps — thank you for keeping us young and reminding us of our own childhood. Swimming ponies in the river, having mud fights, playing Tip 'n' Out are still some of our favourite activities at camp. You can often forget to have these moments of genuine fun as you transition to adulthood, but it's because of you we have realised that you can't always take life too seriously. We hope we have helped each of you develop the same passion for our equine friends as we have, and have encouraged you to never stop chasing your dreams — because we know firsthand that anything is possible, no matter your circumstances.

Coming next . . . Don't miss Book 2 in the
Showtym Adventures **series**

CAMEO, THE STREET PONY

The adventure continues — training a STREET pony into a SHOW pony!

When eight-year-old Kelly Wilson outgrows her 11-hand pony, her mum surprises her with a steel grey mare, which she has seen trotting through town, tied to the back of a rusty old truck. Cameo is the most beautiful pony Kelly has ever seen, but there's a catch — she has never been ridden!

Unsure about training a young pony of her own, Kelly challenges her older sister Vicki to help out and is inspired by the arrival of a top show jumping rider. While Vicki and Amanda compete in their first show jumping class, Kelly is starting from scratch, teaching Cameo the basics of being ridden. Will Cameo ever be ready for jumping competitions? And will this common street pony hold her own against the purebred show ponies at the Royal Show?

An uplifting true story of setbacks and success from the Wilson Sisters' early years, in which Vicki, Kelly and Amanda Wilson first experience the thrill of competition and succeeding on ponies they trained from scratch.